THE GAVEL AND THE GUN

JACK R. STANLEY

Wrightbridge Press

The Gun and the Gavel

Text copyright © 2016 by Jack R. Stanley.
All rights reserved.

ISBN: 978-1-947726-52-9
Wrightbridge Press

jacks@wrightbridgepress.com
http://www.jackrstanley.com

As always, to the love of my life,
Mary Lee.

CHAPTER 1

Three cowboys sat on the ground around a small fire in a steady drizzle.

"Hello, the camp!" a call came from out of the dark.

All three cowboys leap to their feet with their pistols in their hands.

"Who's there?" the eldest man of 30 with a full and bushy beard yelled back.

"A pilgrim on his way home to Texas," came the response. "For a place at your fire, I'll share my coffee and some beans!"

"Come in slowly," the cowboy leader said after exchanging looks with his fellow riders. "Gun belt over your saddle horn and your hands in the open."

"I'm unarmed — but I'll come easy."

The rider approached slowly on a tired-looking roan. He held his reins high in one hand and the other hand away from his body, fingers spread.

"How come you ain't armed?" the lead cowboy said suspiciously.

"I'm a circuit-riding preacher. Spent the winter up in Kansas with a trail drive — but I'm headed home now."

The rider stopped in the dim light of the hissing fire. His hat drooped on all sides, and his slicker covered most of his body. He looked up into the sky, saying, "The Lord sends the rains on the just and the unjust."

"Amen," said one of the cowboys putting his six-gun away.

"I am grateful but wet and tired," the rider said. "Still, what I have I am willing to share."

"Then climb on down and pull up a rock," the second cowboy said, putting his pistol back in its holster. "We're headed south, too. Hopin' t' make Texas tomorrow."

"We're back from trailin' longhorns up to Sedalia."

"If you could stand the company," the preacher said, "I'd take it as a kindness to ride along with you."

"You're welcome," the bearded cowboy said, lowering his pistol but not holstering it. "Climb down and come get yourself warm."

"Bless you, friend," the preacher said as he angled his roan, so it was between him and the cowboys as he dismounted. "But I promised coffee -- and I got a few beans," he said, reaching into his saddlebags.

As the preacher placed a hand on his horse's rump and walked around the animal, he appeared with .45 Colt in his hand. Without another word, he shot the bearded leader who still held his pistol at his side in the center of his chest. Before the other men could react, he turned and repeated his deadly aim on the other two men, throwing them backward to mud puddles.

The camp was silent for a moment as the *"preacher"* tipped back his hat to reveal a nasty scar across one eye and down his right cheek.

"They're all dead, boys!" he called into the night. Two rough-looking men rode in wearing slickers.

"Ace, you get the horses," their leader ordered. "Will and I will check t' see if these fellow's left anything worthwhile for us."

The pair dismounted. Ace, the skinny hook-nosed one, held his gun in his hand as he made his way to the hobbled horses.

"There's four horses here, Rosco!"

"And there are four saddles on the ground," added the other standing near the fire. This one pulled his pistol. "And one of these men is still alive."

"You know what to do, Will," Rosco said.

Will fired twice. "*Was alive*," he said.

"Bring the horses and throw saddles on each one. If there's another cowboy out there, we'll kill him, too, if need be!" the "preacher," Rosco, said loud enough to be heard anywhere nearby.

The one called Ace brought the horses down to the fire. The thin framed man glanced at the dead cowboys on the ground.

"When you kill a man, Rosco, make sure he's dead 'fore you walk away." Shaggy headed Will Hoxie pulled his holstered revolver and fired once. He hit one of the dead cowboys in the head. "Now, that's the way it's done."

The three killers mounted up and rode out, leading the four riderless horses.

Back in the rocks, a 17-year-old cowboy named, Dell, watched with his black-powder pistol in his hand but was too scared to make a sound.

Fifty-one-year-old Ottis Vanderhoff showed his age, the ravages of being on the losing side in the war, and trying to hack out a life as a half-breed farming in the Indian Territory.

He could still do a full day's plowing in the field he had left fallow last year when he turned his mule, Ruff, around and started another row. Three black men stepped out from behind a bush as Ottis pulled up on the reins and faced the three.

"Uziel," Ottis said, addressing the group's leader. All were obvious former slaves, but Uziel was a big lazy man. "Thought you said you'd never set foot on this land again. You back looking for work?"

"I ain't your slave no more, Ottis," the angry man spat out.

"No," said Ottis, "but I have no more to offer you now than I had before — food and a roof over your head. We've got no money. We're just tryin' t' stay alive. And there's only enough work for one -- not you and your friends."

"I ain't come t' beggin'."

"Never thought you did."

"You owe me. You owe all of us!"

"I was always fair to you, Uziel. You ate what we ate and had as good a shelter as we had."

"But I slept in the barn!"

"I have nothing more t' offer you now." Ottis looked at Uziel's two partners. "We can offer your friends a meal — but there's not enough work for them."

"We didn't come to work," Uziel said, glancing at each of his partners.

"This is a dry land farm. That's all there is. If you don't want t' work — I've got nothing for you."

Ottis turned back to his mule and popped the reins.

Uziel leaned down and picked up a flat rock. With a vicious blow, he smashed it into the back of Ottis's head, breaking bone and splattering blood into the dust. Ottis was dead before his knees hit the furrows.

Inside the farmhouse, a full-blooded Choctaw woman,

Lutie, Ottis's wife, was baking an apple pie when she heard heavy footsteps on the back porch.

"Who gave out first? Ruff or you, Ottis?" she joked as she wiped her hands on her apron. "And don't you even think of trackin' those dirty boots into my kitchen."

When she looked up, she saw the big black man standing there with two others behind him.

"Uziel? I thought once you got your freedom, we'd never see you around these parts again?"

She approached him, looking around his huge frame.

"Where's Ottis? You should have seen him out in the north field."

"He ain't there no more," Uziel said with a slightly cruel smile.

"Where is he?" Lutie asked, pushing him aside and stepping outside.

"Same place you goin'," he said, bringing a hatchet down and splitting her skull open. "T' hell!"

The woman fell to the planks and didn't move.

Uziel's friends stepped over her body, and the three men went inside the house.

"Come on, Bart! You're almost there!"

Tollie worked hard at her job, and she was good at it. She was the best whore in Muskogee Maude's "Big House" for almost five years since her husband, a clerk, had been killed in a bank robbery there. This was the only job she could get that would keep her and her son, Bobby, fed, clothed, and a roof over their heads. She had grown up in an orphanage and was willing to do anything to keep her child from knowing that same fate.

Bart Zolan was an overweight, mid-40's, hairy lump of a

man — too drunk to focus on what he was doing. Finally, Tollie stopped and climbed off of him.

"Do you want to try again in a minute — when you're rested up?"

"Hell, no!" he said, reaching for the bottle on the bedside table.

Tollie wrapped herself in the top sheet and went to the dresser to wash up.

"Come on, Bart. I'm tryin' my best here."

"I don't give a damn. You're just a whore to me."

"Damn you, Bart Zolan!" she said, turning on him. "This ain't the first time you've quit on me. You don't finish, I don't get paid." She dropped the sheet. "Let's try again!"

"Then here's your pay, bitch!" He grabbed his .44 Remington out of his holster hanging on the bedpost, pulled back the hammer and shot Tollie between her breasts.

The room rang with the thunder of the blast inside the closed space. But a few moments later, there were footsteps on the upstairs hallway outside the door. Men carrying pistols and Henry repeating rifles, in long johns and Levi's, all without boots, gathered near the door.

"It came from in here," one voice said as Zolan shoved his feet into his boots and buckled his belt. Bart fired two shots through the door before snatching up his dirty shirt and climbing out the window and onto the balcony. He was over the rail and sliding down a pole when a rifle shot splintered the door jam and armed men rushed in.

All they found was young Tollie dead, the window curtains moving in the breeze through the open window, and a vest hanging on a chair with the U.S. Marshal's badge still pinned to it.

★★★

A dozen riders holding burning torches against the darkness, their heads covered with flour or seed sacks with a pair of eye holes cut in each, led a single circled rider with his hands bound behind him. This gagged rider was missing one leg from the left knee down. He wore a Confederate Army cap and almost worn out gray rebel Army pants.

The group stopped under a tall tree that had a thick branch extended across the dusty road. One of the hooded men tossed a rope over the branch while another dismounted and swung the end of the line around the base of the tree, ready to tie it off.

Another hooded rider untied the gag.

The guest of this neck-tie party spoke to the other party-goers.

"You can't hang me! I didn't do nothing! I showed you the bill of sale for this horse! I bought and paid for him!"

The leader of the vigilantes rode over and showed the bound man a sheet of paper.

"Yeah," the victim said, "that's it! You can keep the horse."

The leader folded and stuffed the bill of sale into the bound man's pocket while another removed the rebel cap and slipped a loop over his head.

"Hey, that's not even a proper hangman's knot. That will choke me to death!"

Once the loop was secured and tightened around the victim's scruffy neck, the rider at the foot of the tree tied off the rope. The line was tight and rubbed against the man's throat as he sat up in the saddle.

"This ain't right!" the suspected horse thief said. "What kind of men are you to hang an innocent man without a trial?"

The vigilantes backed their horses up away from the man in the saddle with the rope around his neck. Then slowly, they walked their mounts back the way they came. It was only after they were away from the tree that the riders urged their horses into trots and then gallops.

The bound man was left alone with the rope over the branch and tied to the tree sitting on his mount.

"Cowards!" he shouts, and his horse starts to move. "Whoa, girl," he says gently to the horse.

The man sat there as the vigilantes rode away, and he was left in the silent night, knowing he would live only so long as his horse remained still.

CHAPTER 2

T he stern-wheeler Queen of the City tied up at the docks in Ft. Smith. Sitting on the dock on a bale of cotton waiting to be loaded aboard was a balding man holding a bowler hat in his ink-stained hands. He had mutton chops and two days' growth of beard on his 40 year-old-face. He peered over his wire-rimmed glasses at the first passenger to come down the gangplank.

It was a big man, 6' 5" in black military boots, blue pants, and a cavalry hat without any insignia. With deep blue eyes, auburn hair, and a square jaw, the man looked confident and had an air of authority about him. But he was not threatening even though he wore a big flap covered revolver in a cross draw holster on the front edge of his left hip.

"Welcome to Ft. Smith," said the man stepping down from the cotton bale and extending a hand. "Claxton Landers," he said, "reporter, editor, owner of *the* Ft. Smith Daily Ledger."

"Mr. Landers," the tall man said. "Mace Truax. Pleased to meet you."

"New people in town are news," Lander said, producing a

folded piece of paper and a pencil. "Mind if I as you a couple of questions."

"Nope," Truax said.

"What brings you to our fair frontier town?"

"I'm low on funds. And have a desire to continue to eat."

The newspaperman laughed.

"I do understand that, Mr. Truax," he scribbled a note on his piece of paper. "You're late of the cavalry unless I miss my guess. I say -- an officer?"

"That I am -- or was. But the Army's got more captains these days than it needs. I've been killing Indians since before the war in Texas -- and then out West with the Army. They're like ants and flies. You can't kill'em all. I decided it was time for me to move on to something else."

"Anything in particular?"

"At the moment, I'm looking for an honest poker game. My poke could use a little refreshing."

"Try The Sidewheeler -- center of town. You can't miss it. They don't put up with slick gamblers."

"I'll do that." Truax tipped his hat, "Mr. Landers."

"Thanks for your time, Mr. Truax."

Another man, squat, sweat-stained shirt, and green eye-shade on his thinning hair, hurried up out of breath. He was in his early 50's and wore a sour expression.

"Who was that?" he panted, watching Truax walk up the hill.

"You can read about him in tomorrow's edition," Claxton said.

"Bastard."

"Pick, if you had gotten here first, would you have told me?"

"Go t' hell, Claxton."

The editor laughs and says, "He's a fellow just out of the Army looking for a poker game to make some money."

"No carpetbagger judge, yet?"

"Is that the way he'll be characterized in The Vindicator?"

"We report the truth."

"Or at least your version of it."

"There he is," the older man said, pointing up to a passenger without a hat. "See, carpetbagger."

The man stepping down the stairs from the stateroom to the main deck was average height, a full head of dark brown hair, a mustache and goatee. He wore a black three-piece suit, and in his hand, he carried a round handled walking cane and carpetbag.

"Made up your mind already have you, Pick," Claxton said. "Give the man a chance. He can't be worse than Judge Story. Even you called him corrupt."

"Story's gone, and this jasper is who we'll have to deal with now."

"Might not be a bad idea to start out on his good side."

"He's a Yankee. That's enough for me."

"The war's been over for 10 years, Pick. Even you should be reconstructed by now."

"Never!" the older man said. "He was a Lincoln Republican -- and Grant appointed him judge. Yankee."

The new judge shook hands with the steamboat captain who tipped his hat, and the judge stepped down the gangplank.

"Judge," Claxton called, but the jurist didn't respond. The editor tried again, "Judge Issac Parker!"

Parker looked up at Claxton.

"You'll have to excuse me. I'm not used to the title quite yet."

"I'm Claxton Landers -- editor of the Ft. Smith Daily Ledger."

The Judge shook hands with Claxton.

"My pleasure to meet you, Mr. Claxton."

"This is my competitor, Mr. Joseph Pickering, editor of The Vindicator."

"I can speak for myself," Pick says.

"Good afternoon, gentlemen. What can I do for you?"

"You're Grant's Yankee judge, right?" Pickering asked with a sneer.

"I am the new Federal Judge for the Western District of Arkansas -- appointed by President Grant and confirmed by the Senate -- as are all Federal judges. As for being a Yankee -- no, I consider myself an American."

"And what are your plans for Ft. Smith and the Indian Territory?" Claxton cut in.

"I intend to bring justice and fairness to everyone in this jurisdiction."

"Judge, there's a popular saying -- 'There's no Sunday West of St. Louis -- and no God West of Ft. Smith.'"

"Perhaps that was true in the past -- but this is a new day."

"You believe one man can make a difference?" Pickering jabbed his short pencil at the judge.

"Judas Iscariot was one man, Mr. Pickering, but so was Simon Peter. Of course, one man can make a difference. And a tree is known by the fruits it bears. I hope to be judged by my actions."

"What about your marshal?"

"A mister -- Zolan, I believe? What about him?"

"Your honor," Claxton interrupted Pick's questioning, "there's evidence he shot and murdered a young woman in Muskogee -- over in the Territory."

"A whore," Pick added. "He got away, but he left his badge behind."

"I'll issue a warrant for Mr. Zolon's arrest."

"You won't find any deputies ready to take up that warrant."

"Then, I'll appoint a new marshal who will."

"You are ambitious, I'll give you that, Judge," Pickering said.

CHAPTER 3

A carriage pulled up, driven by a man in his late 30's, short, thin, blond-haired, wearing a suit. The man climbed down, removing his bowler hat.

"Judge Issac Parker?" he asked.

"Yes," the judge answered.

"Sir, I am a Presley Cross, your court clerk. I apologize for my tardiness. The stable owner didn't have the carriage ready when he had promised."

"I appreciate you coming to get me, Mr. Cross."

"I'll see to your luggage, Your Honor."

"Thank you, sir," the judge said as Cross hurried up the gangplank.

"This man Zolan," the judge continued to the two reporters/editors, "is to be considered innocent until proven guilty. That's the way everyone charged with a crime will be treated in this court."

"That is if he ever gets to court," Pickering said.

"He will, Mr. Pickering. My goal is swift and honest justice."

"Hell, Judge, there hasn't been a trial here in two years."

"We don't even have a district attorney to prosecute cases," Claxton said.

"It seems I have a lot of work to do."

Cross returned leading two men who carried trunks and bags which they deposited in the carriage.

"I have secured you a room at our best hotel, Your Honor. We can deliver your belonging there, and then I can show you the court if you like."

"Very much, Mr. Cross. Thank you for your efficiency and attention to detail."

Cross didn't appear to know how to respond to these compliments.

The judge climbed up in the seat beside Cross.

"Can I offer you gentlemen a ride to town?" the judge asked the reporters.

"Not me," Pickering said.

"Thank you, no, Your Honor. There are other places I need to visit to see about news. We appreciate the offer."

"I"m sure I'll be seeing you both again soon," the judge said, nodding his head.

As Cross drove the wagon, Judge Parker got his first look at the frontier town. The main street was wide but certainly not paved. Rutted and dusty, it was typical of western towns. There were two banks, and there were several merchant buildings, wholesales shops, shippers, and an abundance of saloons.

"Tell me about Bart Zolan," he said, looking around at the buildings and the people.

"A bully and a braggart. He liked his authority, and he liked to hurt people. To your predecessor, Zolan was a good marshal."

"He's certainly not the kind of man I want in the job."

After a moment, the Judge asked, "How many deputy marshals do we have."

"We are allotted two hundred but we have never had more than half of that on the payroll."

"Is it true then none will pick up the warrant on Zolan?"

"No warrant has been issued. Based on witness statements, one of the deputy marshals's collected, I've drawn it up, but it awaits your signature."

"We'll go to the office shortly, and I'll sign it." They rode on a moment more before the Judge said, "Tell me about these marshals."

"A deputy is paid $150 plus $2 per live prisoner he brings in -- 6 cents a mile for travel and he has to pay to feed his prisoners and must pay for the burial of any he kills."

"None of them wants the warrant for Zolan. I've asked. Whoever takes that job will have to be willing to go after Zolan himself."

They passed the Sidewheeler Saloon, a liquor and card palace, which was maybe a little cleaner looking than the average Western saloon.

"At the Sidewheeler -- there -- tonight. Every attorney in town will be there.

"For what?"

"A reception -- to welcome you, Your Honor."

"Good. I'll see what I can do about lining up a persecutor.

After some of the judge's bags were unloaded at the hotel Le Flore, Mr. Cross was ready to take his passenger to the courthouse. However, before they could move, a barred wagon with five prisoners in it passed by.

"Where are they going?" the judge asked.

"To the jail. It's attached to the courthouse, Your Honor."

A lawman rode a dappled gray gelding behind the wagon. He wore buckskin pants and a faded cotton shirt and no hat.

"Is there a deputy who you'd recommend for the Marshal's job?"

"Heck Thomas -- but he's out serving warrants. Could be a month or more before he returns."

"I don't think we can wait that long. Who is that deputy?" the judge motioned toward the retreating rider with the wagon load of prisoners.

"He's not a deputy. That's John Browneagle -- Indian Police -- Choctaw Lighthorse in his case."

John Browneagle was not an imposing man, just over 5 feet 8 inches tall, with straight black hair and deeply tanned skin. But there was something confident about the way he carried himself.

"Lighthouse?"

"That's what the Indian Police force is called He operates somewhat under your jurisdiction, but he's the Indian Agent for his tribe."

"Somewhat?"

"He works for the Five Civilized Tribes. But Browneagle is one of the best."

"I want to see the jail."

"Before you do, Your Honor, there's one more thing I'd like to show you."

"Lead on, Mr. Cross."

The carriage headed down the street and out of town.

"Where I'm taking you, Your Honor, is a place called The Hanging Tree. It's been used by vigilantes in these parts for years."

"There will be no more of that, I assure you, Mr. Cross. Vigilante justice is no justice."

"It's better than nothing -- sometimes better than the justice coming out of the courthouse. I'm speaking of your predecessor."

"We must send a strong message, Mr. Cross -- and quickly that there is justice here -- as well as law and order."

The two rode on in silence until the judge turned to his clerk.

"Mr. Cross, there's something stuck in your craw. I would be obliged if you'd spit it out. If we're going to be working together, I think frankness should be the order of the day -- every day."

"Well, for one thing, we're *not* going to be working together."

"I beg your pardon?"

"I've been the clerk for this court for eight years and under three different judges. One is now a territorial governor, one is in Congress, and the last was this close to being put on trial himself. What I've seen I would not call law, order, or justice."

"Go on."

"I am very aware of what your new position pays, and it is hardly what I'd call the job of a lifetime from someone who'd studied the law and who had the influence to obtain such an appointment. It's a stepping stone -- a short stop along the way for someone who has greater ambitions -- not an end unto itself."

"I assure you, Mr. Cross, you'd be surprised how little *influence* it required. There wasn't a line of applicants for this position."

"I happen to be a man of principals, Your Honor -- principals which I believe surpassed those of anyone I've seen on this bench. I was a school teacher but choose to take the job of court clerk because I hoped to make a difference. I love the country and the people I've gotten to know here -- but I can make more of a difference in a classroom than I can in the courthouse."

"Then why have you stayed so long?"

"Hope. I have hoped against all the evidence I've seen that a jurist will ascend to this court and make some real changes. I'm no quitter, but as soon as you are settled into your job, I will be leaving."

"That sounds very noble, Mr. Cross, but it appears to me that *quitting* is exactly what you are doing. I'm not here on my way to anywhere else. I came to Ft. Smith and to this court to dispense justice. Your help is appreciated for as long as you decide to stay, but please don't pass judgment on me based on what you've seen in the past."

The carriage rounded a curve on the wooded road, and Cross pulled the horses to a halt. Ahead of them sat a man astride a horse with a rope around his neck.

CHAPTER 4

"Whoa -- back, girl," the lean man on the horse croaked out as he used his one good leg and his wooden peg to urge the animal to back up.

"Slowly," the Judge said to his driver as the two men stepped down to the ground.

"Please..." the man with a rope burned neck whispered as loudly as he can.

"Go cut the rope at the base of the tree," the Judge said as he approached the horse.

"I have nothing to cut it with," Cross said.

The Judge pulled a pocket knife out of one vest pocket and unhooked it from the gold chain, which connected it to the watch in his other pocket. He tossed the knife to Cross, who caught it and opened the blade.

"Steady," the judge said to the horse as he approached. The animal stepped back and strained the rope in the other direction. Judge Parker stopped, and so did the horse.

Cross reached the tree and began sawing through the threads of the rope, but it was not going very fast.

"Remind me to keep that knife sharpened, Mr. Cross."

The horse shook its head and snorted as the Judge began to move again.

"Whoa," the desperate man squeaked out.

Suddenly the horse bolted, and the judge rushed forward and grabbed the man by the legs as he slipped from the saddle. Cross kept sawing and finally got through the rope. The hanged man's full weight fell on the Judge, who then eased him to the ground.

The man gasped for air as the judge removed the rope.

"Do we have a canteen?"

"There's one on the horse."

"Get it."

For some reason, the frightened horse allowed Cross to approach and take the canteen off the saddle horn. The clerk patted the animal and quickly brought the water to the judge and the victim now on the ground.

The man drank several gulps from the canteen.

"Do you know who he is?" Judge Parker asked Cross.

"His name is Stonewall Welch. Hard case -- former Confederate. See, he still wears part of the uniform." Cross looked around. "Usually he wears the cap, too. They call him 'Stoney.'"

"Lost my leg at Chickamauga," the exhausted man rasps with pride. "We sure kicked the Yankee's ass that day."

"Who was trying to hang you?" the judge asked.

"Didn't introduce themselves," Stoney Welch managed to say.

"Why did they do this to you?"

"Stealin' my horse. But I got the bill of sale in my pocket."

"There was a shooting in one of the local saloons two nights ago," Cross said. "This man killed a gambler named Tom Bartlett."

"Crooked gambler. And a fair fight. He drew on me."

"Bartlett did have a less than stellar reputation."

"Damn straight."

"As to who drew first -- there are differing opinions on that."

"Then I'm placing you under arrest, Mr. Welch," the judge said, helping Stoney to his feet.

"Arrest? Fer what? I'm th' one's almost hung."

"Manslaughter -- perhaps even murder. We'll have to see."

"Who the hell are you?"

"I'm Judge Issac Parker."

"The new District Court Judge," Cross added.

"Don't worry, you'll get a fair trial, that I can guarantee."

"And then you'll hang me -- again?"

"If you're found guilty."

"I ain't guilty. I told you the son of a bitch drew on me."

"That's for a jury to decide. Get yourself a lawyer."

"Lawyer? With what? Them vigilantes took all the money I had left."

"Then, the court will see to it that you have an adequate defense."

"Adequate? Hell, I need a miracle! Half th' men in this town are Yankees!"

"The war is over, Mr. Welch."

"Not for me."

"It will be if you're hanged," Cross said.

The jail had three levels. Connected to the old barracks building, which served as the courthouse, the two-story brick building sat on a whitewashed stone foundation and basement. All windows were barred, and a slanted walkway led from ground level down to the jail's lower level.

Judge Parker and Mr. Cross ushered Stoney Welch down the ramp to the jail where they were met by Herb Irwin, jailer, and chief guard. The pale-skinned, overweight, hulking man with beady eyes took the new prisoner and led him to a cell.

"This place stinks," Judge Parker said, wrinkling his face.

"It'll get worse as the summer drags on," Cross told him.

When Herb Irwin returned, Judge Parker said, "Mr. Irwin, I want you to clean this place up. There is no reason for this stench."

"It's a jail, Judge. It ain't supposed to be a hotel."

"And each man here is innocent until proven guilty. Clean it up!"

The courthouse was an old two-story, converted military barracks, perhaps it had been a former headquarters at some point. It had a porch, several windows, and an overall official look about it. But the building was in disrepair. Spokes were missing from the porch and stair railings. Weeds also thrived around the plank front steps.

Judge Parker and Presley Cross mounted the stairs, stepped across the porch, and pushed open the double front door. A set of stairs led to the upper floor. On this floor, though, there was an anti room, and beyond that, an empty courtroom with benches for observers, a dozen chairs for the jury, and at the rear of the space, a dust-covered judge's bench.

The Judge walked down the center aisle of the room and paused to wipe his hand across the railing that separated the gallery from the rest of the court. He looked at his hand. It was dusty. He threw a disapproving glance at Cross.

"There didn't seem to be much point in keeping it clean. The place was never used -- like I said -- for two years."

Judge Parker shook his head and walked across to look at the jury box, scanning the empty chairs from one end to the other.

"That's another problem," Cross said. "The juries. It reached a point where they were never paid -- or if they were -- it was as much as a year later."

The Judge turned to face Cross.

"I have some money, Mr. Cross. I want you to set up an account with the biggest local bank. Pay the jurors out of that -- reimburse me when Washington finally gets around to it."

"You might want to think that over, Your Honor."

"There's nothing to think about. We will have no court unless we have juries -- jury service is a civic duty, but jurors deserve to be paid for their time."

Cross shrugged. "Whatever you say." He made himself a note.

The Judge crossed over and examined the judge's bench and chair. It, too, was dusty and held a neglected gavel. Cross moved over to the door behind the bench, which led out of the courtroom to a back staircase.

"The offices are up this way."

The Judge crossed to the door and followed Mr. Cross up the stairs.

CHAPTER 5

"**T**his will do very nicely," Judge Parker said, examining what would be his office. There were a large desk and padded high back chair, two windows, a work table, wall to wall bookcases, all empty at the moment, and two visitor chairs near a fireplace.

"Your books will be delivered tomorrow," Cross said. "I talked to the steamboat's captain."

The sound of footsteps was heard coming up another staircase. Cross went through the door to his adjoining office and opened the outer door. The judge continued to look around his space.

A figure stopped in the judge's door and then turned back to Cross. At first glance, it was difficult to tell if this visitor was male or female. On a second look, it became evident that it was a woman. She was dressed in men's clothes, and while somewhat attractive, she was dirty. The woman was in her early 30's.

She spoke to Cross, who stood behind the door he had opened to allow her in.

"There you are, you little weasel," she stepped over to

Cross and shook her finger in his face. "You *told* me he'd be in today -- and --." She stopped and whipped around on the Judge again. "You that there new judge?"

The woman had an attractive figure, even her clothes couldn't hide. Her hair, which needed a good wash and combing was black as her eyes.

The Judge found this woman interesting. He stepped across his office to her.

"I am. Judge Isaac Parker. I'm afraid you have the advantage of me, madam. Who are you?"

She let out a deep belly laugh. She was still laughing when she managed to speak. "I've worked in a couple of houses -- but I ain't no *madam*."

"I beg your pardon. I meant the term as one of respect, not of derision."

"*Derision*? Damn, but you must be a judge usin' words like that." She extended a small calloused hand to the judge. "I'm Bell Starr."

"Is it Miss — or Mrs?"

Starting to laugh again, she said, "Hell, honey, it's jest Bell."

They shook hands.

"Bell," the judge said after a moment, "is there something I can do for you?"

"Damn right there is. Get Uriah Starr out of your hoosegow."

The judge didn't grasp what she was saying. He turned to Cross standing behind Bell in his office.

"Uriah Starr -- this woman's -- common-law husband -- and...."

"He's my husband -- all legal as can be"

Judge Parker reacted to this in surprise but focused on Cross to make it clear.

"Husband -- then?"

"I don't give a damn what ya' call 'im, I jest want t' get him out."

"What are the charges against this -- Uriah Starr?"

"The same as always -- bootlegging."

Bell spoke up again, "Tell your judge about my -- whatever you call that thing Temple Houston fixed up for me?"

Cross was displeased with this, but he sighed and explained.

"Mr. Temple Houston -- whom you will meet tonight -- drew up a writ of habeas corpus. It seems all the evidence against Mr. Starr -- *mysteriously* -- disappeared."

"Ya' might say it was magic. But that's nobody's never mind. Ya' got nothin' t' prove he done nothin'. So you got no right t' keep him locked up in that damn 'stink hole down there."

"I've been telling her that no one could act on this -- except the new judge."

Bell turned to the judge.

"S' you're th' new judge -- and you're here an' so am I. Now let's get Uriah out."

"Would you please give the man a chance. He hasn't been in town a full day, yet. Tomorrow will be soon enough."

"Th' hell, it will!" Bell bellowed.

Judge Parker said, "Mr. Cross. Let me see the writ, please."

Cross made a face, glared at Bell, and then turned to his desk.

Judge Parker motioned to one of the visitor chairs.

"I'm afraid everything is little dusty -- Bell --but have a seat."

"Hell, I don't mind a little dirt."

She sat, leaning forward, her elbows on her knees like a man. She watched the judge as he went around behind his desk, pulled out a pair of glasses, and cleaned them with his handkerchief.

After a moment, Bell spook again.

"Talk is you're an Indian lover, nigger-lover, and you're a carpetbagger."

The judge stopped cleaning his glasses and looked up at Bell.

Bell threw her hands up.

"Hey -- I don't give a damn. I had a brother killed by the rebs -- my first husband was a damn Yankee. They shot him fer desertin'. I was raised by a mammy who was black as th' ace a' spades -- an' th' man I'm livin' with -- Uriah -- he's part Shawnee. I'm jest tellin' you what people are sayin'."

Cross stepped back into the judge's office carrying a two-page legal brief. He went over to the judge and handed him the pages. The judge accepted the brief, he put on his glasses and read the document quickly as Cross gave Bell a dirty look.

After a couple of moments, Judge Parker looked up and took a second look at the top of the document.

"Temple Houston. Sam Houston's son? He practices in Ft. Smith?"

Cross turned back to the judge, frowning as he spoke.

"If he's not too busy playing cards -- or getting himself debauched at one of the local -- cat houses."

The judge nodded.

"This is well done."

Bell got to her feet speaking.

"Th' best is all I'll get fer anybody 'works fer me. Now, how's about it? You lettin' Uriah out?

Judge Parker looked evenly at Bell for a moment, then stood and turned to Cross.

"Will you get me a release form, Mr. Cross?"

Cross sighed and produced one which he brought in with him.

"All it requires is your signature, Your Honor."

The judge looked for a pen. There was not one on the desk. He opened a couple of drawers before he found one, then dipped it in a bottle of ink and signed the paper. He blew on his signature to dry it and handed it to Cross. Cross didn't like it, but he handed it to Bell.

She looked over the form nodding as she did. She adjusted her hat and stepped up to shake hands with Judge Parker again.

"It's a pleasure doin' business with ya', Judge."

He shook hands with her, reluctantly.

"A word to the wise -- Bell. Evidence had better not disappear again."

Bell laughed.

"Don't tell me. I had nothin' t' do with it.

"I'm sure."

There was an awkward moment during which Bell was aware that her attempt to laugh this off did not work. She decided to become her usual hostile self.

"Listen, I got other fish t' fry and pigs t' stick. Ya' mind if I get about it?"

"Not at all. Good day."

"Yeah," Bell said as she threw a sarcastic and victorious smile at Cross and then left.

Judge Parker put his glasses up and reached for his watch. He checked the time and looked back up to see Cross glaring at him.

"Mr. Cross, is there something you'd like to say. I don't believe we finished our conversation in the buggy."

"Your Honor, I happen to be a man of principle."

"Yes, you told me that."

"Is what just happened the kind of justice you plan to dispense -- allowing the likes of Uriah Starr to go free?

"Justice, Mr. Cross, is blind. She treats all men the same. There was no evidence with which to try Mr. Starr -- be he innocent or guilty. Without it, he does not deserve to be in jail."

"This kind of thing will make you very popular with certain elements in these parts."

"I did not come here to be popular. Neither, as I told you before, did I come here expecting to step from this position to another political post. What if it had been you instead of Mr. Starr in jail and no evidence. How long would you feel it just to keep you incarcerated?"

There was a silence between the judge and his clerk.

"Mr. Cross, your knowledge and assistance are greatly appreciated -- for however long you decide to remain in your job. But don't you take your toys and run home blaming anyone but yourself if it takes longer than it should to get things straightened out. If you are interested in justice, I suggest you button up your courage and get back to work. Court opens at 8 o'clock tomorrow morning -- and I expect this place to be clean."

The judge crossed to the door with Cross watching -- the clerk's mouth open but no word forthcoming. The judge stopped before he left.

"Please call for me at my hotel -- if you are still disposed to introduce me to the town's attorneys tonight. If not, I'll find my own way."

The judge walked out, leaving Cross in the empty offices when he encountered a young cowboy, hat in hand outside in the hall at the Marshal's closed door.

"Can I help you?" Parker asked.

"I was lookin' fer th' Marshal."

"I'm afraid we don't have one at the moment. What do you need?"

Mr. Cross heard the conversation and stepped out behind the judge as the young man said, "My name's Dell -- Dell Maguire. I'm a cowboy from Texas."

"All right," the judge said, trying to be patient. "Why did you need to see the Marshal?"

"The three men I was ridin' with --," he swallowed before finishing, "-- they was murdered in our camp -- about a week back. It's taken me this long to get here afoot."

"Do you know who killed them?"

"I heard them use the names -- Rosco, Ace -- and Will."

"Could be Rosco Dury," Cross said as he stepped forward. "He calls himself 'preacher' sometimes."

"That's what they called him," the young cowboy said.

"He rides with Ace Keogh and Will Hoxie," the clerk offered.

"Could you identify these men if you saw them again?" the judge asked.

Dell nodded his head and tightened his jaw. "I'll never forget them faces."

CHAPTER 6

The editor of the Ft. Smith Daily Ledger, Claxton Landers, stood at the bar in his rumpled suit, enjoying a beer with a merchant in a business suit. The businessman finished his drink, shook hands with Claxton, and left. Claxton tilted back his bowler hat and turned to the activity in the saloon.

From one of the side rooms, Mace Truax, the first passenger to emerge from the Queen of the City riverboat that morning, stepped out pocketing a wad of greenbacks. The tall, former army officer went to the bar and took up a position beside the newspaperman.

"CaptainTruax," Claxton began stroking his mutton chops, "I see you found your poker game."

"That I did," the former soldier said in his deep voice. "And did all right -- for a while."

"Let me guess. You met a man in a white suit and hat -- a mustache. Then your luck seems to change."

"How'd you figure that?"

"Oh, I've seen it happen before. I'm thinking you were smart enough to get out while you were still ahead."

"Let's say I got out while the gettin' was good."

Claxton Landers chuckles. "Not everyone is so wise."

"Three or four hours ago, I was doin' pretty well. Then that fella' showed up."

"Figure he's cheating'?"

"If he is, I'll be damned if I can see how."

"He's not. You just met Temple Houston."

"Sam Houston's son?"

"That's him."

"Hmmm. I use t' work for his ol' man, Governor Sam."

"How's that?"

"I was a Texas Ranger 'til the war was over. I was on the Texas Indian frontier."

"Let me buy you a drink," Claxton said.

"I can pay for my own, now," Mace said.

"It's a gesture of friendship."

"Accepted."

"Jules!" he called the bartender. To Mace, he said, "What's your pleasure?

"A beer would suit my pistol just fine."

"Two beers.

"Comin' up." the sandy-haired barkeep said.

When the brews arrived, Claxton proposed a toast. "To you, Captain."

"Make it, Mace. I'm shut of the Army for good."

"To you, Mace Truax."

"And to you, Mr. Landers."

"Claxton."

"Claxton."

They drank.

"I'll tell you something," the editor said, setting the beer down. "Temple Houston doesn't cheat. Doesn't have to. He's simply that good at reading other people."

"Well, he read me well enough."

"Mace -- I've seen Houston win $5,000 at that table in one night."

"Five thousand?"

"And when the game was over, he told the other man what his *tell* was. The man agreed and left without a word. The next night Houston was back and lost it all -- and then some."

"You don't say."

"Made a believer out of me -- at that same table, once. Cleaned me out. Told me, 'Don't bet it if you can't afford to lose.'"

"That's been my rule," the larger man said.

"So you goin' back to Texas?"

"Oh, I don't know. Stories I've heard about Texas since the war don't sound all that inviting, t' me."

Just then, the sound of shattering bar glasses came from behind Claxton. He and Mace turned.

Two cowboy types, dirty, rough, big, and over half-drunk, Dutch and Coy, had squared off at each other a few feet away from the bar. Dutch, the larger of the two, had a big bowie knife in his hand, ready to slash Coy, who had pulled his cap and ball pistol.

"I'm goin' t' gut you, Coy. Slit you open like the hog you are!

"Like hell you are, you lying' piece of shit! I'm goin' t' blow your fool head off -- leave your ears with nothin' t' hang on to!"

Judge Parker and Mr. Cross, both clean and in fresh clothes, stepped into the saloon and stood watching by the front doors. Everyone else in the place was also focused on the two drunks.

"You ain't goin' t' do nothin'!" Coy declared.

"Oh, yeah, Dutch?!!"

Coy, swayed in his tracks, used both his thumbs to pull back the hammer of his weapon.

But before Coy could pull the trigger, Mace pulled his pistol from his cross draw holster and smashed it across Coy's face -- causing him to drop the weapon. As almost a continuation of the same move, Mace slammed the barrel down on Dutch's knife holding arm. The force of the blow drove the blade into the board floor -- point first.

"You broke my arm!" Dutch shouted.

"If I didn't, it wasn't for lack of tryin'."

The judge took note of Truax and his ability to handle this situation as the barkeep produced a double-barrel shotgun from under the bar.

Coy held his face, blood streaming through his fingers, and looked for his pistol as Truax stepped over and snatched it off the floor. Claxton saw the shotgun and said, "I don't think we'll be needing that, Jules."

The bartender glanced from Coy to Dutch and then back before he nodded and lowered his weapon.

Coy turned to Mace.

"Hey, who the hell are you?"

"A friend."

"You ain't no friend of mine," Coy said on unsteady feet.

Mace motioned to the two combatants.

"How long have you two known each other?"

It was Dutch who spoke up. "We been ridin' t'gether fer twenty years."

"Closer t' twenty-five," Coy said.

Mace looked at Coy.

"Would you say *he's* a friend."

"Damn right!"

"Well, I just kept you from killing your friend."

Coy realized what Mace had just said and looked at the two weapons the tall man held in his hands.

"You boys come t' town t' get drunk -- and fight?

"Sure. What else?" Dutch said. "I wouldn't have cut him."

JACK R. STANLEY

"And I weren't goin' t' kill Dutch. That ol' hogleg don't even work half th' time."

Mace Truax spun the chambers of the pistol, executed the road-agent's-spin, cocked it, and fired it into the floor.

Coy was shocked.

Mace pulled on the end of Dutch's hair and whacked off a piece with the razor-sharp knife blade. Then turning to the barkeep, Mace said, "Put these somewhere safe -- but don't give 'em back until these two are ready to leave town."

"Will do."

"Why don't you help your friend find a doctor?" Mace suggested.

Coy and Dutch nodded, and headed out the door, sheepishly.

"And you boys do th' rest of your drinkin' an' all your fightin' -- somewheres else," the bartender called after them.

Judge Parker stepped aside to let them exit. The judge nodded his head to Cross. The Judge indicated Truax.

"Mr. Cross, please find out who that man is. I would like to talk to him -- tomorrow."

Claxton patted Mace on the back. "Nice work there."

Truax shrugged it off.

"Half of the job of an officer in the Army was to keep the enlisted men from killing each other when they got bored."

The bartender sat two more beers on the bar.

"On th' house," he said. He offered his hand to Mace. "Call me, Jules."

"Thanks," Mace and Landers echoed each other.

Mace raised his glass to the bartender, "Jules. I'm Mace."

Presley Cross stepped up to the bar, saying, "Excuse me, sir."

CHAPTER 7

A meeting room in the back of the Sidewheeler was filled with suited lawyers, about fifteen in all, of every size, shape, and age. The judge was working the room shaking hands with each in turn.

Mr. Cross arrived and stepped in to introduce the various attorneys to the judge.

Cross was saying, "...had a distinguished career in Maryland before coming west.

The judge shook hands with this lawyer, saying, "I look forward to working with you."

The attorney was gracious. "It will be my pleasure, Your Honor."

The last man in line at the head table was clean-shaven, had deep-set, narrow eyes, and a severe face. The forty-year-old was Rupert Dalby.

Cross said, "Rupert Dalby is the president of the local bar association."

The judge took Dalby's hand.

"Mr. Dalby."

Dalby was a humorless man who projected an air of over

self-confidence. It felt as if he believed he had a wonderful voice, and everything he had to say was of earth-shattering significance.

It didn't take Dalby long to get to his main point.

"Your Honor, I would like it known from day one that I expect to be the District Attorney for your court."

The remark caught Judge Parker off guard. Yet, he managed to nod calmly and refused to commit to anything.

"I see," he said. "I will be appointing a temporary prosecutor. The position, however, is not mine to fill -- permanently. As you know, it's federally appointed."

"Of course. But we all understand that a recommendation from Your Honor will certainly carry the day and make the appointment virtually *pro forma*. It is our belief," Rupert Dalby swept his hand to include everyone in the room, "that you need to recommend a prosecutor who knows this territory and who is familiar with the criminal element here. Western Arkansas and the Indian Territory has become a haven for the very worst of human scum. Unless drastic and sustained action is taken, we might as well hand this land back to the savages."

"There are, of course, those who would claim that such is exactly what has already happened."

"I dare *say* you won't find the name of Rupert Dalby among them. Despite everything, some of us believe progress has been made here -- although often without the help of our court."

"That's good to hear, Mr. Dalby. But I will decide whom to recommend -- and unless that person is you, sir, you won't find your name with the title of Federal District Attorney for my court, either."

Dalby was taken aback by the judge's stance.

Judge Parker went on, "Ultimately, the position will be appointed by President Grant."

Dalby didn't know what to say to this.

It was Presley Cross who broke up the potentially volatile encounter by raising his voice so all could hear.

"Gentlemen! Would you all please have a seat!"

Lawyers began to sit down, and Dalby took one of the chairs at the head table. Judge Parker took a step forward and began to address the gathering.

"Is everyone here?" he asked, looking around.

"Everybody that matters," Dalby spoke under his breath.

"Gentlemen. There are a great number of rumors going around about me and what I stand for."

There was a slight mummer from the crowd.

Judge Parker moved on.

"I do not intend to deal with rumors or any attacks which might be aimed at my person from the press --," he noted squat, early 50's, editor Pick Pickering. "To para-phrase our late President Lincoln -- I will do the best I can do. If I were to address every objection this office will receive, I might as well close the court to any other business."

There was another rumble from the crowd.

"While I sit on this bench -- all I can do is my best as I see it. I will do the very best I can. At the end of my days -- if my actions bring me out all right, then what is said against me won't matter one hoot in hell. But if those actions bring me out wrong -- a dozen angels sitting on my grave, swearing I was right -- will make no difference."

There were some nods and other reactions to the judge's words.

"Justice -- fair and impartial justice is the business of this court. Not vengeance -- not retribution -- but justice. Anyone brought before my court is first of all -- considered innocent until proven guilty. Second -- any such person -- he or she -- is equal, free and entitled to the protections and limitations of the same laws." Judge Parker paused and looked around the room before continuing.

"I want to make sure you gentlemen all understand *that* from the very beginning."

The lawyers reacted to this with a mixture of emotions.

"Now -- the first major piece of business of this court will be to select a *temporary* District Attorney."

The judge cut his eyes to Rupert Dalby.

"It's my understanding that Mr. Dalby is interested in the post. Are there any others?"

Dalby got to his feet, glancing around to make sure there were no discouraging reactions against him.

"Your Honor, this Bar Association has already endorsed me for that position."

"Excellent," Judge Parker said.

"But not unanimously."

All heads turned towards the door.

Standing just inside the door, in all his white suit and hat, and wearing a black gun belt was Temple Houston. Houston stepped forward.

"As I recall -- the vote -- if we can call it that -- was rather -- contested."

Houston continued to walk forward until he was close to Dalby.

"A vote was taken -- and it is final! I'm the president of this association."

Houston brushed his thin mustache as he said, "Were that you were -- emperor -- then there would be no reason for such messy things as votes. A simple 'Off with their heads' would quell any problems -- or opposition."

Houston turned and stepped up to the judge, offering his hand.

"Your honor, I've not had the pleasure. Temple Houston -- at your service."

"Mr. Houston," the judge said, taking Houston's hand.

"Do I take it that you are also a candidate for the position?

Houston threw a glance back to Dalby.

"I wouldn't say 'no' if it were offered, Your Honor." Turning back to the judge, the attorney finished. "Steady employment would be a real boon to me."

Dalby was fuming.

"Do you think you could leave the poker table and the cat houses long enough to come to court?" the head of the Bar Association asked.

Back to Dalby, Houston said, "It would depend primarily on what the charges against you were, Dalby."

The room erupted with laughter as Dalby continued to burn slowly.

The judge watched this exchange and let the laughter die down before he spoke.

"I will keep the association's recommendation in mind -- but I intend to make my own independent recommendation. To that end, in the coming weeks, I would like to see every attorney interested in practicing in my court -- to do so."

Another murmur flowed through the room.

Going on, the judge said, "Court will be open six days a week -- beginning tomorrow morning. There are a sufficient number of cases to allow every one of you gentlemen ample opportunity to demonstrate your skills."

Houston nodded his head to this.

Dalby didn't -- but there wasn't much he could do. The other lawyers found the possibilities interesting.

"I need a defense attorney for the very first case in particular. It's for a man the local vigilantes tried to lynch last night."

The lawyers exchanged looks and mumbled, and the name "Stoney" was heard.

"I would be pleased to prosecute that case, Your Honor," Dalby spoke up.

Once more, the judge was caught by the unexpected for a moment.

Houston turned to the judge.

"In that case, I will gladly defend the case."

This surprised everyone in the room.

"All right. But, Mr. Houston, I accept your offer -- but you should understand that this particular defendant says he has no money to pay. Will you still accept the case on a *pro-bono* basis?

"I did very well at the tables tonight, Your Honor. I'll take the case -- *pro bono* -- for the sake of justice.

CHAPTER 8

T he old courthouse was full for the first trial in two years. Rupert Dalby acted as the prosecuting attorney. In his early 40's, the lean and narrow-faced lawyer with thinning hair almost strutted in front of the jury wearing his best-starched collar as he made his closing statement.

"Murder! A man's life ended by the violence of a bullet which tore through his chest and ripped open his heart!"

Judge Parker, in his official black robes of office, was as attentive as any member of the jury. He scratched his dapper chin whiskers once or twice but never lost his focus on attorney Dalby's words.

"We have seen this kind of killing too many times in the streets of Ft. Smith -- and the killer walks free because it is claimed to have been a *fair fight*. Killing a human being with a gun is murder! It is something civilized men must not permit!"

Dalby pointed at Stoney Welch, who sat with his peg leg under the defense table, next to his attorney, Temple Houston.

"That man, Stoney Welch -- gunned down -- *murdered* -- Tom Bartlett!

It was obvious that Stoney didn't like Dalby and frowned at the strutting, prattling prosecuting attorney.

Houston, in his usual white suit and black boots, took notes as Dalby went on.

"It is up to this court and to you gentlemen of the jury to stop this slaughter in our streets! If any of you hope to raise a family in this territory -- make a home here -- you must put an end to this kind of senseless killing -- and send a message far and wide that murder will not be tolerated in Ft. Smith!"

Dalby turned again to Welch.

"We must stop this kind of violence and the men who perpetrate these crimes as a part of their way of life."

The attorney turned again to the jury.

"Today has been his day in court -- his chance to express his views -- something Tom Bartlett will never have. Stoney Welch has had a fair trial -- and now, if you gentlemen will do your job, he will have his day with the hangman! Then, and only then, will we start to clean up this town and this territory? It is up to you!"

Dalby scowled a moment before he turned and crossed back to his table, saying, "Your Honor, the prosecution rests."

Presley Cross was busy taking notes as the judge spoke.

"Mr. Houston. Your summation, please."

Temple Houston confidently nodded and stood.

"May it please the court." He strode over toward the jury box. "*Gentlemen* -- how many of you have been called that before?"

The men in the jury find that funny and laughed.

"Now let's talk about my client -- Stoney Welch -- a man most of you know. Some of you like him, and some of you don't. None-the-less, Stoney is a man who -- like many of you

-- took up arms in the recent war where he suffered the loss of a leg."

"At Chickamauga," Stoney said proudly. "I may have lost a leg, but we sure kicked the Yankee's ass that day."

This remark elicited hoots, claps, and boos from members of the jury as well as observers in the gallery.

"Order in the court!" Judge Parker shouted as he banged on his bench with his gavel. "Mr. Houston, if you can't control your client, I will have him removed!"

"Your Honor, my client is a proud man, and the day of his life-altering injury will always be a powerful memory for him."

"Not while he's in my court!"

"Forgive him, Your Honor -- members of the jury." Temple continued with the jury, "How many of you can even imagine what such a loss would be like? He has had to make his own way in this world -- against odds, most of us know little to nothing about."

Temple gestured toward his client.

"Wounded -- then imprisoned in Andersonville -- the name itself speaks of its own horrors. In that God-forsaken hell hole -- he had his left leg amputated because the butchers there could offer him no better medical treatment."

The attorney paused and let these words sink in.

"And now -- maimed -- disfigured -- handicapped -- jobless -- he has to compete in the world with all the able-bodied men -- just to survive. Stoney Welch -- in spite of what the prosecution would have you believe -- is an honest man. He gets by as best he can -- working at whatever jobs he can get -- usually jobs no one else wants. How many of you men in the jury have offered Stoney a job?"

Temple Houston looked over at his client as he said, "And, too, he takes his chances at the poker table -- trying to make what little money he has into more."

Judge Parker was listening as carefully to Temple as he did to Dalby.

"You all knew Tom Bartlett -- or knew of him."

"Objection!" Dalby lept to his feet. "Tom Bartlett's character is not on trial here. And he is not here to defend himself."

"Your Honor," Temple said calmly, "I've said nothing derogatory about Mr. Bartlett. It was his life as a cheat and a liar that preceded him wherever he went."

"Objection!"

Temple said to the jury in an offhand way, "Even if he were here, there wouldn't be a whole lot to defend."

Some members of the jury chuckled and nodded their heads at this.

The judge rapped his gavel again.

"Objection sustained. Mr. Houston, deal only with the facts -- and not with the character assassination of a dead man."

"Of course, Your Honor," Temple said as Dalby sank back into his seat.

"Let's talk about what happened the night Stoney ran into Tom Bartlett," winking at the jury so that the judge could not see it.

"Stoney Welch sat down and was playing a game of seven-card stud with Tom Bartlett. I hope the court doesn't consider it disrespectful to say that Tom Bartlett was known to be fast and deadly with his own two pistols. It is a fact that in the past year, Mr. Bartlett was involved in gunfights with three other men -- and those men are all dead. Does the prosecution wish to dispute that fact?"

Dalby sat stewing at his table but did not object.

"Stoney Welch could have been number four -- except that he was faster than Bartlett."

Houston backed away from the jury.

"Now Mr. Stoney Welsh claimed Tom Bartlett shot first. Other men who were there differ in their opinions. Some say Stoney had his gun out before Bartlett even went for this gun. So how could he have shot first?

"Remember that Derringer stuffed up Bartlett's sleeve. Yes, that pistol was unfired -- but only because it jammed. Is it possible, as my client tells us, that the gambler pulled his hide-away gun first, but it didn't work? Then while he crammed it out of the way, Stoney drew his gun and fired before Bartlett could get his revolver out of his holster?

"Imagine if you will -- that you were the one across the table from Tom Bartlett and you caught him cheating. There you stand, face to face with a man who wore one pistol -- but had another up his sleeve?"

Temple walked up and down in front of the jury.

"Have any of you ever been shot before? Stoney has. Do you know what it feels like to have your flesh and bone shattered by an ounce of lead? Can you imagine that in a split second you could be -- unable to walk at all -- blinded -- even dead? Can you imagine the feeling of facing a man who can do this to you?"

Houston yanked his pistol from his shoulder holster and shot over the heads of the jury.

The members of the jury were at first shocked, then frightened, and began to scramble for their lives.

Judge Parker, too, was in shock and thrown back in horror.

Dalby all but wet his pants as he dropped to the floor and hid under the table with his hands over his head.

Temple continued to fire.

Half the jury dove out the windows at each end of the jury box. Other members of the jury scrambled through the crowded courtroom, making for the double doors.

Temple emptied his gun and returned it to his holster under his coat.

The judge was irate. On his feet, he shouted at Temple.

"Mr. Houston!! What are you doing!! Put that gun down!! I find you in contempt of court!"

Temple looked up innocently at the judge.

"Of course, Your Honor."

"That little stunt will cost you one hundred dollars."

"A hundred dollars?!! This is already a pro bono case."

"Mr. Cross! Get the jury back in here!!" Judge Parker continued to hammer on his desk.

It took nearly half an hour to regather the jury and get them all back in their seats. Some were angry, others at least shaken, all rattled as they took their seats.

"I wish to apologize to the members of the jury for the shock and the inconvenience of my display," the defense attorney said once the proceedings began again.

Temple turned to the judge and said, "And I apologize to the court for the commotion."

This didn't seem to do a lot of good, but after a few moments, Temple Houston continued.

"We are talking about a man's life here. And as far as I'm concerned, nothing is too extreme to make a point where a man's life is on the line. I was using blanks -- and no one was ever truly in danger. But you didn't know that. Tom Bartlett was not using blanks. Stoney Welch was fighting for his life. I ask you to remember in your deliberations -- just what it felt like when a man with a gun was shooting at you -- perhaps trying to kill you. If you'd had your guns, what would you have done?"

Temple took another moment to look at the jury, even though the members didn't seem mollified. Temple turned and crossed back to his client.

"The defense rests, Your Honor."

"That was damn good," Stoney says quietly to his attorney as Temple took his seat.

The judge addressed the jury.

"The jury may now retire to consider a verdict."

The jury stood and started to move out, grumbling as they went. But before the last man has disappeared into the Jury Room, the group stopped and returned.

Judge Parker didn't know what to make of this.

Dalby was also surprised.

Temple Houston and Welch had been talking together but stopped and looked up as the jury filed back in.

The jury got back to their original seats. The foreman stood up.

"Your Honor, we got our verdict."

The judge was still taken aback. He shook his head to try and get a grip on reality.

"You have? All right. What is your verdict?

The foreman turned to Temple and Welch.

"We find th' son of a bitch, guilty!"

Dalby, of course, was very pleased. Stoney Welch felt like the world had come to an end, and the crowd erupted in mummers. Houston held his hand up to Welch as if to say, "Just wait." Houston stood.

"Your Honor! Your Honor!"

The court settled down a little as the judge rapped on his bench.

"What is it, Mr. Houston?"

"Your Honor, I move to have the jury's verdict set aside and call for a directed verdict from the court based on the facts."

Dalby didn't believe this.

"Set aside?!" Dalby said, lurching to his feet. "He's crazy!! The jury had reached its verdict, and I demand Your Honor proceed to the sentencing of this killer!"

Judge Parker felt a headache coming on. He rubbed his head a moment and banged on his bench for quiet before he spoke to Houston again.

"On what grounds do you make your motions, Mr. Houston?"

Dalby was aghast.

"You are not going to listen to him, are you, Your Honor?"

Stoney didn't know what was going on, but he was hopeful that his attorney had something good up his sleeve.

Temple stood his ground and spoke with total confidence.

"Your Honor, the jury was not sequestered during the course of this trial. Members left the jury box mingled with the crowd -- talked about these proceedings to those not directly involved with this case -- and therefore no longer constitute a legal jury."

Dalby is outraged at this. But he couldn't find a legal argument to make. He stammers but makes little more than noise.

"I object!! The jury was running for their lives! It was Houston's fault that they left the jury box."

"While my learned opponent may be correct, Your Honor -- the fact remains regardless of the cause -- or the blame -- the jury was not sequestered as the law requires. This can be corrected one of two ways -- impound a new jury and we retry the case -- or Your Honor makes a ruling based on the facts of the case."

Dalby was was not prepared for such logic.

Judge Parker considered the argument for a moment and then made his pronouncement.

"Mr. Houston, your legal point is well taken. Jury dismissed."

There are rumbles from the crowd.

"I hereby rule that in this matter, based purely on the facts and evidence presented, that Mr. Welch is innocent.

Case dismissed." The judge bangs his gavel. "You are free to go, Mr. Welch."

Welch was excited and leaped up, shaking Temple's hands while Dalby stood fuming.

"Mr. Houston," the judge says, "please see the court clerk to pay your contempt fine. "This court is adjourned until 2 o'clock this afternoon, at which time we will take up the next case on the docket."

The judge rapped his gavel.

CHAPTER 9

"Have a seat, Mr. Truax," Judge Parker said as he entered his office and removed his robe. The jurist placed his robe on a wooden coat hanger, which he then hung inside an armoire. The big man sat down across the desk from where the judge took a seat.

"We didn't have a chance to meet the other night in the Sidewheeler, but I saw the way you handled those two men in what could have evolved into a deadly situation."

Boxes of books were all around the office, with some already beginning to take up space on the shelves.

"Have you read all these books?" Mace asked.

"Not all. Most are for reference -- precedencies from other court cases -- both here and abroad." The judge watched Mace a moment as his visitor looked around the office. "I read in one of the local newspapers you have experience as a Texas Ranger and was an officer in the Army following the war."

"You've got your facts right."

"You went to West Point?"

Mace nodded as his reply.

"And you were recently retired from the military? Honorably, I presume?"

"Right again."

"Would you be interested in a job as a U.S. Marshal?"

"U.S. Marshal? Now there's something I never thought about."

"I was hoping you'd consider the job. You seem to have the qualifications."

"What exactly does the job encompass?"

"There is one marshal in charge of up to 200 deputy marshals and a dozen or more Territorial Indian Police to cover over 72,000 miles of jurisdiction."

"Indian Police?"

"They work for the Five Civilized Tribes in the Indian Territory -- but also for this court. Some matters they settle within the tribes because the matters only involve other Indians. Whites and Indians who commit crimes against whites are brought back here for trial."

"So it's a desk job. Not what I'm looking for at all, I'm afraid."

"The job is whatever you'd make it, Mr. Truax. There is an office for the Marshal down the hall here -- and there would be some paperwork involved -- but the position of supervising deputy marshals and Indian Police officers would demand -- whatever that requires."

"I'd about decided I'd had all the Army I wanted. Seems to me this would be like tradin' a uniform for a badge."

"It all depends on who the man is who puts on the badge. First of all, you would answer to no one except me -- and the law. The only time we'd see each other is when you had a question or you were testifying in court as a witness. The rest of the time you would be supervising deputies and Indian Police. You would hire and fire any deputy under you -- oh, and you would also be responsible for the jail. I've just ordered the current jailer to bring that facility up to decent standards."

Mace was thinking about it.

"That sounds like there's a lot of -- authority -- and power behind this office of marshal."

"Then you do grasp the significance of the position. But that is why I am interested in a man with your experience -- and what I judge to be -- common sense, Mr. Truax." The judge opened his drawer and put a used, but shiny six-pointed star with the words "U.S. Marshal" stamped into the metal.

Mace studied the badge as the Judge went on.

"You impress me as a man with a level head. This territory doesn't need a marshal who would hide behind this badge -- or flaunt it -- but a man who will make it stand for something."

Mace finally looked up at Judge Parker.

"I'm not a lawyer -- never have been. I don't have shelves of books to carry around to know what is and isn't the law."

"Did you know the law when you were a Ranger?"

"'Didn't have t'. It was just right and wrong. We protected the good people of the Texas frontier against the Apaches and the Comanches -- and the gun runners and crooks who tended to flock out there."

"You have pretty much just defined the marshal's job -- if you throw in whiskey runners along with the gun runners -- and the addition of the paperwork and the jail I spoke about."

The judge reached into his top drawer and pulled out a single sheet of paper.

"This is an arrest warrant."

Truax took the document and read it.

"Bart Zolan. Who is he and where do I look for him?"

"He was the last man to wear this badge -- he brought it nothing but dishonor and shame. I understand that his warrant is one none of the deputies available are willing to take on. According to witness statements, he killed a young woman in Muskogee."

"Muskogee. I think I'm going to need a map -- or a guide."

"Do you have any objections to working with an Indian? A policeman."

Mace was silent for a moment. His jaw tightened before he spoke.

"I'm what you might call an Indian fighter, Your Honor. It's what I did before the war and in the Army. I've done about all of that I want."

"The Five Civilized Tribes are not at all what you're used to, Mr. Truax. For the most part, they have adopted our ways. Many have been lied to and mistreated for years and generations. Those who have made peace and live in the Indian Territory deserve our justice."

Mace thought about the judge's words and looked at the badge.

"Is there something you're not saying, Mr. Truax?"

With a sigh, Mace prepared to tell his story.

"My brother-in-law was killed in the Battle of Palmito Ranch -- South Texas -- over a month after Appomattox. They didn't know the war was over. He left behind his wife, my sister, and two little girls. They had nothing and nowhere to go. They've been living with me ever since -- in what was left of our family farm at first. Then they went West with me after the Academy -- lived on each Army posts I was assigned to."

It took Mace a couple of breaths before he could say the rest.

"While I was out on patrol, our outpost was attacked by the Sioux -- overrun. Everyone was killed -- scalped -- and the women raped -- regardless of their age."

"I am very sorry to learn this, Mr. Truax," Judge Parker

said, truly moved. "Have you managed to come to terms with it?"

"I don't know, Your Honor. After that, I did some things I am not very proud of -- but it didn't change anything -- didn't bring them back. And nothing I was going to do in the Army was going to alter the past."

"That's part of the reason for your leaving the Army," the judge said as a statement of understanding rather than a question.

Mace nodded.

"And are you willing to give this marshal's job a try?"

Mace looked at the badge and picked it up for a moment.

"This *isn't* exactly what I had in mind -- but .... What if I try this on for a while? See how it fits -- and how I fit it?"

"It comes off much easier than it goes on, Mr. Truax -- especially if you're not the right man for the job."

"That's kind of the way I'd like it."

"You haven't asked about the salary?"

"If it's anything like the rangers or the army, it'll be fair -- but low -- and both late and slow in coming. I wouldn't take the job because of the pay."

"Let me swear you in, and we'll make this official."

Mace got to his feet and met the judge at the end of the desk, where Judge Parker had picked up a copy of the Holy Bible.

"Left hand on the Bible and raise your right hand."

Mace put the badge on the desk and did as instructed.

"Do you, Mace Truax, swear to uphold the laws of the Western District of Arkansas and the Constitution of the United States of America, so help you, God?"

Mace slowly nodded his head before he answered, "I do."

"Congratulations, Marshal Truax," the judge said, putting down the Bible, picking up the badge, and pinning it on Mace's shirt.

Mace looked down at the badge for a second. Then he glanced up at the Judge.

"There are a few things I'll need -- a horse -- a saddle -- a rifle."

"My clerk will see that you get what you need."

"Okay, then -- I'll try," Mace said slowly.

"When you return, let's talk again."

Mace nodded his head.

To Mace, Judge Parker said, "Bart Zolan -- he is a bully and a vicious killer. Perhaps you may want to take another deputy with you."

"Do I have one?"

"Perhaps that should be your first order of business. Find one."

Court Clerk Cross tapped on the door before opening it and stepping in.

"Mr. Cross is the legal clerk for this court," the judge explained.

"We met last night," Mace said. "Good to see you again, Mr. Cross."

"My pleasure I assure you, Mr. Truax."

The two men shook hands.

"I need you to arrange for Marshal Truax to get a horse, saddle, rifle and whatever other supplies he may need to apprehend Bart Zolan."

This revelation came as a surprise to Cross.

Judge Parker continued, "That Indian policeman you pointed out yesterday -- "

"John Browneagle."

"Yes, John Browneagle. Do you know where the marshal might find him?"

"I don't -- but I'm sure someone at the Sidewheeler would."

"I'll find out myself," Mace said.

"Can you also find the keys to the marshal's office?"

"Yes, sir."

"Marshal, Mr. Cross is the person you should go to first if you have any questions. But of course, my door is always open to you."

"Well, Judge, I'd like to have more than one warrant -- I'm sure you got some more."

"We certainly do," Cross said.

"I can't supervise men doing a job I've never done and don't know how to do."

Judge Parker had a slight smile to his eyes as he spoke, "Mr. Cross will know which are our most important."

CHAPTER 10

"I can't thank you enough, Mr. Houston," Stoney Welch said, standing at the bar of the Sidewheeler.

"Stoney, my job was to get justice for you. I believe I did that."

"There was a moment there. I thought my own lawyer had got me hung."

"I knew it could go either way -- but I had that ace in my pocket."

"Yes, Sir! And ya' played the hell out of it."

The bartender set down two glasses of whiskey before the pair as Mace Truax stepped in from the boardwalk.

"When I gets me a job," Stoney went on, only glancing at the door, "you'll see some payment every month, Mr. Houston. Probably won't be much -- folks don't want t' hire this ol' reb fer much of anything -- but whatever it is -- I'll be payin' you 'til you say we're even. I ain't fergettin' what you done fer me."

Mace stepped up to the bar down the way from the pair already there. He waited until the bartender tossed his bar towel over his shoulder and approached the new marshal.

"What's that you're wearing, Mr. Truax?"

"Mace, if ya' don't mine, Jules."

"It'd be my pleasure -- Marshal." The slightly overweight, sandy-haired barkeep said. "First drink's on the house. Pick your poison."

"I appreciate the offer -- but it's too early in the day -- and in the job, for me, t' start drinking."

"Good idea. But the drink wasn't from me -- it was from Coy and Dutch. The pair you kept from killin' each other last night. They also wanted me to tell you 'Thanks.'"

Mace shrugged this off. "I'm looking for some information."

"Whatever I can do for you, Marshal. And their offer still stands -- it's paid for -- and I'll give you one on the house for steppin' up and taking the marshal's job. Whenever you're ready."

Temple Houston stepped around his former client and crossed the floor to where Mace stood.

"Pardon the intrusion. May I introduce myself, Marshal, I'm Temple Houston, attorney at law."

"And a better poker player than I am," Mace said. "We met the other night."

"Ahh, I recall. And I heard about the incident with the *two ol' friends*. I would like to offer my hand to you in friendship."

Mace turned and, after a moment, accepted Houston's hand. "Don't expect me to be playin' cards with you again anytime soon."

"I play fair, Marshal."

"I've heard that -- 'have no reason to doubt it. But *once burned -- twice shy*."

A drummer came into the saloon and took his sample case to the other end of the bar before setting it down.

"Excuse me, gents," Jules said and went to see to his new customer.

"I heard you once worked for my father," the attorney said.

"For a while. It was before he resigned as governor – and Texas seceded. We never met -- but I was in the Frontier Battalion up on the Brazos."

"Well, Marshal, in light of that, I'd like to offer you a little advice -- for whatever it might be worth to you."

Mace wrinkled his forehead when he turned back to face the white-suited attorney, not sure he'd understood what the man was saying.

"In my younger days -- before father convinced me I should read law and find a more -- honorable -- profession -- I followed a different line. Although I must say, I've not always found that the law has always been blind -- or fair. Anyway, in those days, I fancied myself a young gunfighter -- a shootist, if you will. What I learned then has served me well -- even though I try to be an honorable man these days."

Mace nodded his understanding.

"It's your holster. I realize you've spent several years doing things the Army way -- but I'd suggest you tuck that flap on your pistol back behind the belt -- unless it's raining. Use a thong to loop over your hammer to keep your revolver in place. It's a lot quicker and easier to remove than a flap."

"Never thought of it that way."

"And think about this -- if you switch to a left-handed holster and put it on your right side -- everybody will think you're a lefty. Then if you can learn to reverse your hand as you draw, nobody will be expecting you to be right-handed. 'Could gain you a whole second in a bad situation."

"You've given this a lot of thought."

"Gunfighters all cheat."

Houston walked around Mace until he had his back to the small front bar window.

"Have you ever seen someone do this?"

Houston used his left hand to reach around and pull back his coat so that he could easily get to the pistol in his tied down holster lower down on his right leg.

"I have."

"Well, take a step around behind me if you would."

Mace did and saw the lawyer had his coat held behind him not by his hand but by the butt of a smaller revolver in a horizontal holster in the middle of his back. Houston let his coat drop back and turned to face the Marshal once more.

"Thanks," Mace said. "I never would have expected that."

"Don't get caught playing straight in a rigged game."

The two men shook hands again with mutual respect.

"You might think about wearing a vest, too."

"Why's that?"

"The pockets of a vest are a good place to carry extra loaded cylinders for your pistol. It's a hell of a lot quicker to change cylinders than it is to reload a spent one. It would also cover up your badge until you wanted someone to see it."

"Maybe you should be the Marshal."

"No. I believe you are the right man for the job. But if I can ever be of service -- as an attorney -- or backing you up -- you'll know where to find me."

"That I will."

Houston motioned for Stoney to join them.

"Marshal, you'll be looking for deputies?"

"Could be."

Houston clapped a hand on Stoney's shoulder.

"Here's a good man looking' for a job.

Stoney stepped forward and offered his hand.

"I'm Stoney Welch."

"What's the rope burn on your neck, Mr. Welch?"

The scars from the rope ran from Stoney's collar up to his ear on his left side.

"Some vigilantes made me guest-of-honor at a necktie party. The new judge happened by and saved me. Then he arrested me and tried t' hang me again. But my lawyer here did right by me. I got this burn before the judge found me."

"The reason I've spoken up for Mr. Welch," Houston said, "is because he owes me. It will be difficult for him to pay if he's not working."

"What can you do?" Mace asked the newly released veteran.

"I've seen those jail wagons -- th' ones they call the *tumbleweed wagons*. I can drive a wagon -- two ups, four ups, and even six ups -- and I cook some. I ain't a great cook -- but if I'm cookin' fer outlaws, my cookin' might be what they deserve."

"You'd also be cooking for me."

"I can fill an empty belly, Marshal. I may not win any prizes, but wouldn't let you starve t' death."

Mace looked Stoney over.

"I can also handle a rifle, shotgun, and pistol -- if'in' I had one -- help keep track of some men you're be arrestin'."

"Where's your hat?"

"The vigilantes took it. I was a rebel cap from the war."

"Well, you'll need another hat and some gear. Go on up and see the judge. He'll have t' give his okay."

Stoney balks. "Whoa. Last time I was in that man's court, I almost got strung up for the second time."

"But you didn't," Houston reminded him.

"You're right -- and I said I was lookin' for a job."

"I'll go with you just in case," Houston smiled at Stoney.

"Where do I meet you, Marshal?"

"The mercantile."

Stoney shook Mace's hand and left with Houston.

Jules had returned.

"You sure about him, Marshal? He's been more trouble since he's been in town than worth a damn."

"That'll be part of my job. Now, Jules," Mace said, changing the subject, "I'm here looking for information."

"There's a lot of talking done within these walls," Jules grinned. "What do you need?"

"There's an Indian policeman named John Browneagle."

"I've seen him around. He's not someone to be trifled with," the barkeep said.

"Do you know where I might find him?"

"He usually camps upriver from town when he's about. Five miles or so. Look for a gnarled oak twisted in with a pine tree on your left. I don't know exactly where he puts his blanket down from there, but it's close."

"Thanks."

Mace turned to go, and Jules called after him, "Two drinks, Marshal. Whenever you say."

CHAPTER 11

U riah Starr, the bootlegger for whom Bell Starr had secured a release from Judge Parker's Ft. Smith jail, was not her first husband. That man was a Texas outlaw who had been killed by a deputy sheriff near the town of Paris, Texas, following a bank robbery. Neither Uriah nor the now dead Weaver Reed, Bell's first husband, was the father of her first child, a daughter named Pearl. That honor fell to handsome Cole Younger, a Missouri outlaw who met and slept with young Bell at the Texas ranch of her father.

Cole and his, brother Jim, were the notorious Younger Brothers. Along with the Dalton Brothers, Grat, Bill, Bob, and Emmit plus Frank and Jessie James made up the James-Dalton gang. Following a disastrous attempt to hold up two banks at the same time in Northfield, Minnesota, all were dead except for Frank and Jessie, who escaped, and Emmit who was wounded.

By this point the pattern for the former Bell Shirley's life was cast. She was drawn to, not just bad men, but men with resentment left over from the Civil War, or hatred against authority.

The attraction of Uriah Starr was that he was Cherokee and a member of the feared and ostracized Starr family. His father, Tom, had been such a scourge to his own people, the Cherokee, that the Cherokee Council made a treaty with old man Starr. The agreement promised the Starrs amnesty for past crimes and a pledge to pay the Starrs to behave in the future. The pact even granted the family a large piece of tribal land along a bend in the Upper Canadian River. By marrying into the family, Bell became an heir to the Starr land and income.

Uriah's ranch was situated under the Hi-early mountain in the Northeastern sixth of the Indian Territory which was designated for the Cherokees. It was unique in that it was well guarded by having a single approach and that was a narrow pass under the view of several defensible caves -- an ideal hideout for outlaws coming and going through the territory.

Still Bell was drawn to the wilder criminal life. She dressed in men's clothes, wore a pair of revolvers and took part in robberies of every type. What became quickly apparent was that the men folk could handle the rough and often brutal work of gun play, threats, and intimidation. What was missing was a guide to smartly pull off their deeds of outlawry and make clean escapes.

But what Uriah did best was to make moonshine -- and what Bell wanted most was a desirable bed companion. She saw to it that the men, in what soon became her gang, were well serviced in Tulsey Town, what was to become known as Tulsa. There *houses of male entertainment* were kept busy. This town as well as Claremore, meaning *mountain with a clear view,* and Catoosa, meaning *between two hills,* became major cattle towns on the trail to Kansas.

What neither Bell nor Judge Parker knew after their first encounter was how many time their paths would cross over the coming years. While she set up her criminal hideout and on-going enterprise, Judge Parker was planning a very different future for Western Arkansas and the Indian Territory.

★★★

"Have you ever taken the oath of allegiance to the United States?" Judge Parker asked as he was putting on his robe and preparing for the afternoon session of court.

"Can't say I have," Stoney said. "When we found out the war was over -- most of us headed home."

"If you're going to wear a deputy's badge for this court, Mr. Welch, you're going to have to sign a pledge."

"Should have knowed. I've been avoiding this for 10 years. Guess it had to end some time."

Presley Cross tapped on the door and entered with a sheet of paper which he sat down in front of Stoney.

"It won't hurt at all, Stoney," his attorney, Temple Houston, said from a few feet away. "The war's over -- and the South isn't going to rise again. You should have figured that out by now."

"Ya' can't keep a man from hopin'."

Stoney sighed as he picked up the pen and shook his head as he signed. Judge Parker picked up his Bible. The former rebel put his left hand on the scriptures and raised the right hand.

"Repeat after me," Judge Parker said, "I -- state your name --

"I, Stoney Welch...."

"Use your given name," the judge told him.

It took Stoney a moment and another sigh before he could say, "I, Stonewall Algernon Welch--"

The judge went right on, "...do solemnly swear in the presence of Almighty God, I will hereafter support, protect and defend the Constitution of the United States and the union..."

Temple didn't hear the rest of the oath as it took all his strength to keep from bursting out laughing -- "Algernon".

A moment later Judge Parker penned a Deputy U.S. Marshal's badge on Stoney and shook his hand.

"Now what do you have to say -- citizen Welch?" the judge couldn't help but rub it in -- just a little.

"Oh," Stoney said flipping up the badge and then letting out a breath, "I was just thinking, Judge -- you know them rebs sure did kick our ass at Chickamauga."

The judge's eyes flared and he pointed to the door shouting, "Get out of my office!"

CHAPTER 12

Mace found the unique twisted oak and pine trees and stepped down, tying up his horse as he looked around. It was a wooded area and from over the rise he could hear the gurgling of a running creek.

He put his hands to his mouth and called, "John Browneagle?"

He waited a moment before stepping off toward the rise.

"Marshal?" a voice came from behind Mace which caused him to stop. He turned to find a man with straight black hair tied behind his neck. The man stood tall even with his short stature of only 5 feet 6 inches. He had black eyes and an air of self-assuredness about him. In his arms he cradled a .44 Winchester rifle.

He wore leather pants and moccasins, a Colt in a holster at his left hip and a large knife on the same belt on his other side. He also wore an Indian Police badge penned to his faded shirt.

"Mace Truax," Mace said without offering his hand to the Indian. "Judge Parker told me to look you up. I have some warrants to serve."

"I'll take them," Browneagle said.

"No, I'd like to serve them myself -- with your help -- if you're willing. I hear you just returned from a job and I don't want to rush you."

"We call it a 'scout.'"

Mace was surprised at the policeman's command of English. There was not a hint of struggle searching for a word or its pronunciation.

"Okay. Are you willing to go back out again?"

"Tomorrow. I would like to meet the new judge first."

"Well, he already thinks very highly of you. Your reputa-tion evidently speaks for itself."

"Why do you want to go? No chief marshal has done that."

"I don't want to ask men to do a job I know nothing about -- and can't do myself."

John Browneagle said nothing for a moment but took the time to consider this new marshal. Finally he nodded his head.

"We will need a wagon -- and a new driver. The last one I had quit."

"Just hired a driver. We'll see if he can do the job."

"I'll be at the ferry at first light -- two days from now."

"Any supplies you need?"

The policeman shook his head."

"First light," Mace confirmed. "Day after tomorrow."

At the general store Mace introduced himself to the jolly owner, Howell Keeling. His pudgy hand was like the rest of him, eager to please. He told Mace there was already an account set up for the Marshal's Service. He understood payment was slow in coming, but for the men who wore the badges, Keeling was more than willing to wait and help in any way he could.

"Mrs. Fross wants to settle her account," a handsome young woman said from behind the merchant.

"Oh. Well, let me see to her. Delta, will you please help the new marshal? Delta Wadsworth, this is Marshal Mace Truax. Marshal, my daughter -- and half owner of the store."

"Ma'am," Mace said tipping his hat.

The young woman wore a wedding ring but was dressed in black. She was an attractive woman with a deep sadness about her. She had deep brown hair tied up in a bun behind her head. Her figure was modest but appealing in spite of her mourning clothes.

"Papa likes to deal with some of the customers himself. I believe he will find a way to discover that lady owes less than what's actually on the books."

Across the store an elderly woman showing the ravages of time and life in the West had opened her purse as the merchant opened his ledger.

"What can I do for you, Marshal?" the young widow asked.

"There will be a new deputy, Stoney Welch, who will shortly be here. Please see to his needs and put his charges on the account of the Marshal's office."

"We can certainly do that."

The items Mace purchased were an extra shirt, a vest, and a blanket.

"Please forgive me if I seem forward, Mrs. Wadsworth, but -- how did you lose your husband?"

"Mrs. Wadsworth," she said thoughtfully. "It's been almost a year now, but I always find myself surprised at that name. Thaddeus and I were only married two months before he was killed. We came West to be missionaries. The very first band on Indians we met murdered Thad as he stepped down from our wagon to offer them a prayer and a blessing. At times it's like a bad dream -- and I have trouble calling up his face."

She shook her head as if to clear it.

"Had not some of the men from our wagon train arrived just then -- I might be dead now myself."

"Or worse," Mace said.

"Yes," she said slowly after a moment.

"You said you came West? From where?"

"St. Joseph. Thad had survived the war and swore to do God's work with the rest of his life."

"Sounds to me like he did," Mace said.

Her expression changed from sadness to a slight smile.

"I've never thought of it that way. Thank you, Marshal."

Mace had his purchases written up and then asked directions to the local gunsmith who happened to be located further down the main street.

★★★

Shadrack Granger knew his trade and his weapons. The hardy, stooped shouldered man with a full beard had a shop stocked with rifles and a display case full of pistols.

"You're the new marshal, ain't ya'?" he asked in a raspy voice.

"Word does get around," Mace said.

"Especially when it's good news like this. I was hopin' I would get to meet you, Marshal." The two men shook hands. "Welcome to Ft. Smith. What can I help you with?"

Mace pulled out his .45 Remington from his flap covered cross draw holster. It was a 1858 Army conversion -- one of the first of the Civil War era percussion era revolvers to be re-bored to fire metallic cartridges.

"I need a rifle -- and a pistol that both use the same bullets. I'm thinking .44 - 40."

The gunsmith examined Mace's weapon saying, "Then you'll want a Winchester -- or the latest Henry -- you'll see I have two of the new Henry models with the wooden fore-stock. As I'm sure you know from being in the Army, the metal magazines on the Henry heated up in a fight. Got too hot to hold."

"I had to use my scarf more than once for that very purpose." Mace walked over and took one of the rifles off the rack and tested it for feel. He then sighted down the barrel. He traded the Henry for a new Winchester '73, the same model Browneagle used -- but put it back and picked up the Henry again. "I think I'll go with the Henry. Feels more my style."

"This pistol conversion of yours has been taken care of well," Granger said examining Mace's pistol. "I can give you a good trade in price for it. You want to stick with Remington -- or could I interest you in something new?"

"What do you have?"

"Well," Granger said reaching into his display case, "I have these Smith and Wesson .44 Russians -- they're brand new. I've already filed off the extra trigger spur and removed the lanyard ring from the bottom of the handle -- most don't seem to like those much."

Laying the rifle down on the table top, Mace picked up the seven inch barreled pistol.

"It's top break," Granger showed Mace, "and it ejects the spent cartridges -- or you can replace the whole cylinder." Granger put two extra cylinders on the counter.

Mace snapped the pistol closed and hefted it in both hands.

"It's accurate," the gunsmith said. "Step out back and try a few rounds." He picked up a box of cartridges as he and Mace walked out the back door. Using a dead tree across the creek as a target, Mace loaded and fired five shots and cut a smaller branch from a larger one plus put two slugs into the trunk of the tree.

"I like it," he said.

"You're a good shot," the gunsmith said. "In some of the gunfights I've seen, it's not the fastest man on the draw but the better shot who walked away."

"That's my thinking."

As the pair headed back inside, Granger said, "It also comes with a 5 inch barrel."

Mace tried the shorter version and checked the feel of both configurations in both hands.

"No," he said. "I'll stick with the 7 inch -- and the Henry."

"Good choices. Anything else you need, Marshal?"

Mace had made up his mind before even coming in and took the cross draw holster off his gun belt. "I need a new holster."

"Right side or cross draw?"

"Right -- and no flap."

"I have this black Mexican style, single strap," Granger said producing a cartridge belt with an attached holster. It had a thong for the hammer and a tie down at the bottom.

Mace tried it on for size. It fit.

Mace strapped the belt around his waist and wore his handgun higher than most. He used to wear his handgun lower when he was a Ranger, but years in the army got him used to having it around his waist. He slipped the revolver into the holster.

"Now," Mace said while pulling the pistol a couple of times, "except for some ammunition, I believe I'm ready to go."

"Want the extra cylinders?"

"Yes. Two of them."

★★★

Mace had one more meeting with Presley Cross before leaving. Mace was looking over his office when Cross rapped on the door frame.

"Mr. Cross?"

"The judge wanted me to give you these," the short blonde man said looking over his glasses and placing a bag on Mace's desk.

Inside the bag Mace found a collection of U.S. Deputy Marshal badges.

"His Honor says you are to do all the hiring of new deputies -- and swearing them in." Cross handed Mace a written out copy of the oath he had sworn before Judge Parker.

"Thank you," Mace said. He put the bag in one of his bottom drawers but took two badges with him. When he looked up, Cross was gone.

CHAPTER 13

Baxter Field was a good looking man, and he knew it. He wasn't nervous about testifying in his trial for rape and murder. The 25-year-old had a thin, dark mustache across his upper lip, which matched the wavy hair that hung just below his ears. He was confident with a hint of a mocking smile he was keeping in check.

His attorney, Brice Nuese, clean-shaven, a pear-shaped man with gray hair, took his seat. He had been pleased with the performance his client had given to their well-rehearsed exchange.

"The witness is yours, Mr. Prosecutor," Judge Parker said.

Temple Houston, clad as always in white, didn't stand but instead sat back in his chair to begin his cross-examination. It was his turn to prosecute a case in front of the judge. This was his audition for the judge's recommendation for the position of Federal District Attorney.

"Is it true what I've been told that you have quite a reputation as a ladies man?" Houston asked.

"I'm not one to brag," Fields said, wiping his mustache to ensure each hair was in place. He spoke with a noticeable deep southern accent with a hint of French in his pronunciations. "But I have sworn to tell the truth -- so I must admit the fairer sex has not been known to avoid my company -- if you take my meaning, sir."

"You're too modest, Mr. Fields. The way it's been told to me, you are a regular Romeo. You dress well and pay attention to your manners."

"What's a gentleman supposed to do?" Fields winked at a young woman in the front row of the gallery. "In New Orleans, we find rude behavior boorish and not to be tolerated in polite society."

"Polite society -- is that what brings you to Western Arkansas?"

"No, sir. It's an opportunity. I am looking for a new start in life."

"This is after killing a man in a duel in the Crescent City, correct?"

"The gentleman, if I can stretch the truth enough not to slander the departed, had slandered my good name -- and I called him to the field of honor for his transgression."

Temple got to his feet, taking a deep breath and seemingly looking at notes on the table before him as he did.

"The -- *gentleman* -- had accused you of taking liberties with his very young sister, is that right?"

Fields sat up, and his demeanor changed as he said, "A lie -- every word of it. He paid for it with his life."

"And his sister -- 13 according to the newspaper account -- how did she react to your actions on the *field of honor*?"

"I didn't think it was appropriate to see her after -- my encounter with her brother. And she didn't look 13 to me or anyone else."

"And the group of gentlemen who escorted you from town -- " Temple picked up a newspaper clipping, "-- with tar,

feathers, and a rail -- did they in any way influence your decision to explore the polite society of Yell County?"

"No, sir, they did not!" Fields grew red from his ears to his
cheeks and pounded the arm of his witness chair. "I knew if I
returned to New Orleans, I would be responsible for the
death of every one of them."

"As you were for the young lady's brother?"

"Objection!" Brice Nuese all but shouted as he heaved
himself to his feet. "The prosecution should limit his questions to matters covered in my client's testimony. Nothing
else!"

"I believe, Your Honor, this previous conduct speaks to
the witness's character and therefore the veracity of his
testimony."

"Objection overruled. But, Mr. Houston, you have made
your point, please move on."

"As the court pleases," Temple said satisfied. "Mr. Fields,
how did your search for polite society lead you to meet Miss
Audra Ebbs? Isn't that mostly forest and farming country?"

"In my travels, I happened to be invited to sup with the
Ebbs family by Mother Ebbs when I stopped for water."

"You spent the night at the Ebbs's farm, did you not?"

"I did. Again at their invitation."

"And did Miss Audra -- *take a shine* -- to you?"

"We both seemed to enjoy each other's company at
dinner, and later that evening, strolling around the property."

"Whose idea was the picnic the next day?"

"Audra's."

"Was she -- or her parents -- aware that you intended to
continue your travels immediately?"

"I certainly made no secret of my intentions."

"And yet, the young woman invited you to picnic with her
knowing that you did not expect to remain?"

"Yes."

"That's an attractive handkerchief you have in the upper pocket of your coat, Mr. Fields. May I see it?"

"Of course," Fields said, handing the white piece of linen to Temple.

"'B.F.' The letters embroidered in the corner," Temple showed the stitching to the jury, "-- does that stand for Baxter Fields?"

"Yes. I had that given to me by a friend in New Orleans."

"Just the one?"

"I had others -- but they seemed to have been misplaced along the way."

Temple walked back to his table and opened a small wooden box there. From it, he extracted a wrinkled wad of cloth which he unfolded. It, too, had the same letters identically woven into one corner.

"Would this be one of them?"

Field's face went white as Temple offered him the second handkerchief.

"Where did you get this?" the accused demanded.

"It was stuffed in Audra Ebbs's mouth when her body was found the day after you left. She had been carried downstream about four miles from the site of your picnic."

Baxter Fields sat back with nothing to say.

"The prosecution would like to enter this embroidered handkerchief into evidence, Your Honor." Temple showed the handkerchief to Judge Parker and Brice Nuese before passing it in view of the jury and placing it on the evidence table.

"So, this picnic," Temple said when he began his cross-examination again -- was it just a fine outdoors meal and then you mounted up and rode off?"

"Yes," Fields said. "Exactly like that."

"There was no after-dinner conversation -- no sweet talk -- no hand-holding, no kissing?"

"Look, she hadn't seen a young man in some time except

wounded and broken men from the war -- or men looking for farm labor jobs. Of course, she was starved for conversation. So we talked a while."

"And did you hold her hand -- did you kiss her?"

"She was very eager," Fields confessed. "I find plenty of women are like that around me."

"And one thing led to another -- I mean, nature took its course, didn't it? She didn't intend to, but before she knew it, you two were -- consummating a relationship which had just begun."

"Some women are like that. They're all innocent and shy -- but when they have the chance ---."

"And when a man such as yourself is there to guide them -," Temple added. Fields didn't answer, so Temple asked, "And after it was all over -- you were ready to leave -- but she wanted you to stay -- stay and do the right thing by her."

"I never promised her anything. But she sat there crying that I had to marry her. Marry? I didn't even know her. And I certainly didn't want to be an Arkansas farmer."

"But she wouldn't stop crying, would she?"

"She started screaming at me! What was I to do?"

"You had to shut her up. What did you do -- stuff the handkerchief in her mouth -- and even that wasn't enough -- so you dragged her to the water and shoved her under -- holding her there until she stopped struggling?"

Tears were streaming down Field's cheeks. "I didn't mean to kill her. I really didn't. But she would *not* shut up!"

"Your Honor, the prosecution rests," Temple said and sat down at his table.

CHAPTER 14

T he Indian Territory was originally divided for the Five Civilized Tribes, many of whom had adopted many of the white man's ways. The Indian Removal Act of 1830 granted the President the authority to designate specific lands for tribes who had accepted defeat or signed treaties with the government. But it was the Indian Intercourse Act of 1834 that screwed the native inhabitants of the growing United States. The originally designated lands, North and East of the Red River, extended into Kansas and Nebraska. But by 1854, the creation of Kansas and Nebraska into territories dissolved parts of the promised Indian lands into the other territories. Tribes other than the original five were also moved into what was left of the Indian Territory.

Each band was to be able to maintain its government and exercise its own laws. But as white settlers continued to move westward, the pressure to abolish the Indian Territory mounted.

The creation of the Western District of Arkansas was just one more way the federal government was extending its reach and control over land pledged to the red men. The various tribes had learned through long and bitter struggles that the white man's army and its weapons were well beyond what any single or even the united tribes could fight. It was a case of either accept or go back to wars they knew they could not win.

While the young were not willing to accept the humiliation and the dishonesty of the U.S. government, the older and wiser leaders had seen the devastation and horror years of war could bring, along with the inevitability of defeat and so struggled to keep their firebrand youth in check. Some had educated themselves within the system of the new reality and made lives for themselves as best they could -- struggling with daily existence and focusing on the needs of their immediate family.

This was the world Mace Truax crossed into on a ferry because no bridges were fording the Arkansas within a hundred miles of Ft. Smith. He, John Browneagle, and Stoney Welch were headed to the Choctaw country, a world Indian policeman John Browneagle knew well, and one Stoney Welch had only skirted.

"You could have been picked for this job," the tall marshal said, leaning against the ferry rail with Browneagle. "I've been told by several people you could have done the job."

"I am a Choctaw. Some of the other tribes might take offense."

"And some white men, too, I suppose."

"If my son were still alive, maybe one day he would have been able to do it. This is not the time."

Mace looked across the fresh flowing water as he said, "You -- *had* -- a son?

"He is dead," the Indian Policeman said -- seemingly without emotion.

"Sorry to hear that," Mace said, looking back at Browneagle. " What happened -- if you don't mind my asking'?"

It took several moments before the deeply tanned Indian spoke.

"Thieves looking for a place to hide out killed my wife and my son."

"Did you ever catch them?"

A few moments later, Browneagle added, "We found them -- dealt with them in our way."

The law stated that each Indian nation could deal with a crime within its territory by its own people or other Indian tribes, according to the law broken. White men and black men were the problems of the U.S. government. Crimes involving Indians, which also involved white or black men, were not within the different tribe's laws. The only other Indian lawbreakers who fell to the U.S. courts and lawmen were those bringing liquor into the territory.

"It wasn't enough, was it?" Mace asked after watching his companion for several moments. "Whatever punishment was dealt out?"

Browneagle turned to Mace and looked at him in a new way.

"Nothing ever will be," Mace said. "No matter what."

They were silent for a bit before Mace spoke again.

"Are our ways any better?"

The Indian didn't answer for a bit.

"Are any ways truly just -- fair?" the redman asked. "What is justice -- getting back to the way things were before? Nothing can bring them back -- or ever will. So, there's no balance there."

"Does that mean the law and justice are just revenge? Is that what we do?"

"Part of it," Browneagle said. "Now, I only go through the motions -- do a job -- eat, sleep -- but I'm hollow inside."

Mace leaned on his side and told his companion. "I know

you won't believe it -- but with time, things do get better. Never back to where they were -- but better."

"I don't think there are any answers," Browneagle said. "The law -- justice -- doing this job -- it may be the best any can do."

There didn't seem to be much more to say. John Browneagle kept a great deal inside him.

They stood in silence as the two ferrymen walked the length of both sides of the barge, pushing poles deep in the water.

"So," Mace said as they approached the far green bank, "don't you resent me for taking the marshal's job -- because it doesn't matter, does it?"

"You did not ask for this job. The judge offered it to you -- and you said you'd try it -- see how it fit."

"What did you think of the judge?"

"He has good words -- powerful words. Only time will tell if he is true to them or not."

Stoney was talking to the horses and feeding them some carrots. The new hat he had picked up at Howell Keeling's mercantile had the brim pushed flat up against the crown as if he were riding face on into a stiff wind. It defeated the purpose of a brim, but Mace kept his thoughts to himself. How a man wore his hat was his own business.

As they waited for the ferry to reach the other bank, Mace found himself thinking about Delta Wadsworth, the young widow in the mercantile. Why, he thought? She was a handsome woman -- but he had seen more appealing -- even fetching women over the years. Why was this one suddenly in his head. He shook it off.

The three lawmen unloaded into the Indian Territory along with four other passengers, two Indians, a black man, and a drummer leading a packhorse carrying his sample cases.

They were in Choctaw land, the lower Southeastern fifth

of the territory. Mounted up, they moved out with Browneagle in the lead. After most of a day's travel, they came upon a wide path of beaten-down grass. It was the Shawnee Trail -- the first of the cattle trails from Texas to Kansas. They were 50 or so miles north of the Red River.

Cut deep into the well-trod and eaten grass were the marks of a heavily loaded wagon. John Browneagle was on one knee, examining the marks and followed them off into the distance with his eyes.

"Wouldn't be the chuck wagon," Stoney said. "It's the first thing ahead of the cattle."

"Guns or whiskey," Browneagle said.

"I guess they were counting on the next herd through to cover their tracks. Too bad for them, we found 'em first."

"Should we trail them a while before we call it a day?" Mace asked.

"With a load like this, they're not going far or fast. We wouldn't catch up with them today -- but if we camp too near, they could smell our fire."

Mace agreed. "What's the nearest town?"

"Durant," Browneagle said, standing and swinging back into the saddle. "They could have a few customers there."

Mace turned to Stoney.

"Let's find a place to make camp. Before first light, I'll go with Browneagle and see if we can find these guys. You follow, and we'll have some passengers for you."

There were no saloons in the Indian Territory. It was against the law to sell liquor there. Pool halls, however, were in almost every town and crossroads.

The heavy tracks of the ladened wagon led Mace and Browneagle to the back door of one such hall. They approached quietly on foot in a gully that ran full whenever it rained. Two men, one muscled and bearded and another shaven and thick through the middle, returned to the wagon, climbed aboard, and pulled away with their only slightly lightened load.

It was too late to catch them in the act, so the lawmen returned to their mounts as the blush of morning turned into clear daylight. Once they were sure of the wagon's direction, Mace and Browneagle made their way around and a good mile ahead of the whiskey smugglers.

At the bottom of a slight hill, John Browneagle staggered out into the road ahead of the wagon, waving an empty whiskey bottle he carried for just this purpose. The wagon driver, the shaven one, pulled to a halt while the other lifted his Winchester at the approaching figure.

"Firewater!" John Browneagle called out, weaving his way up beside the horses.

"Hold up," the driver said to his partner.

Browneagle pulled greenbacks and some coins out of his pants pocket and offered it to the pair on the wagon.

"We can always do a little business," the driver said.

The other man scanned the area with his rifle before he relented and leaned the weapon on its butt near his feet. He turned around and gripped the back of the wagon seat with one hand as he flipped back the tarp covering the wagon's goods. He produced a full bottle. The driver took the money and handed Browneagle the new bottle. The Indian dropped his empty bottle to the dust.

As soon as the exchange was made, Browneagle stepped back and used the thumb of his left hand, the hand holding the bottle, to open the vest he had borrowed from Mace to reveal his badge. At the same time, he pulled his pistol from the waistband of his pants behind him.

"You are under arrest," he announced.

The bearded man beside the driver grabbed for his Winchester just as Mace stepped out from behind a tree and levered a cartridge into his new Henry.

"Don't try it!" Mace called, sighting down his barrel, "unless you're ready to die."

The bearded man let his rifle slip back and raised his left hand, taking hold of the back of the seat as he eased himself down. The driver had both hands up. But the passenger slipped his pistol from his holster hidden between the two men.

Before he could bring the Colt to bare, John Browneagle shot the man in the chest. He was dead as his body fell out of the wagon, bounced off the left front wheel, and hit the ground.

"You want to give it a try?" Mace asked the driver.

"I may not be the smartest child my momma ever raised," the man said with the reins draped across one raised hand, "but I damn sure know when my luck's run out."

CHAPTER 15

The town of Muskogee began as a French fur trader's village on a tributary of the Arkansas River. In 1817 the first permanent European-American settlement was established on the south bank of the Verdigris River -- the name came from the Spanish words *verde,* and *gris,* meaning "green" and "grey." A gray-green substance resembling a copper ore colored the water and was the reason for the name.

One of the Five Civilized Tribes forced into the Indian Territory under President Andrew Jackson in the 1830s was the Creek -- Muskogee is a corruption of the Indian word for Creek. They took their slaves to their new home and built a two-story stone building in Muskogee. Here was the site for meetings among the leaders of the Five Tribes.

The Missouri-Kansas-Texas Railroad reached the town in 1872. Thus the town became a rough place filled with slaves freed following the war, cowboys, railroad men, and all that came with such a congregation. Pool halls instead of saloons crowded the dirt or mud-covered main street, and houses of ill repute openly plied their trade.

The lawmen approached the town wearily. There were two wagons now. Having hitched the whiskey wagon to the back of his tumbleweed wagon, Stoney now drove the horses four up. They made camp outside of town, and their single whiskey running prisoner sat inside the rolling jail. They had buried the dead whiskey trader near where he fell.

Mace and Browneagle were able to locate Uziel Washington in the third pool room they tried. The tall, heavyset former slave sat drinking out of a dirty looking glass at the back of the hall. Mace and Browneagle split up and approached the table where two companions were also drinking and laughing with the big man.

Mace stepped up to the empty chair at the table and spoke.

"Uziel Washington?"

All three men looked up, but no one said anything as their leader looked Mace over.

"Why ya' askin'," Uziel finally said.

"Do you know a couple named Vanderhoss -- Ottis and Lutie Vanderhoss?"

"Used to. They're both dead now."

"How do you know?"

"Cause I kilt 'em both."

"Then I have something for you."

Uziel sneered as he said, "Well, ya' found me. What ya' got that I'm interested in?"

Mace reached inside his vest and extracted the warrant for Uziel's arrest. He handed it across the table.

"I don't read," Uziel said. "So, ya' jest wasted y're time," he wadded up the paper up and threw it at Mace. The document hit him in the chest and dropped to the tabletop.

"Not really," Mace said, picking up and straightening out the paper. He folded it and put it back in his vest. "This is a warrant for your arrest for the murder of Ottis and Lutie Vanderhoss. I'm takin' you back to Ft. Smith to stand trial."

Uziel laughed in an ugly gag. He lunged to his feet as Mace gripped the edge of the table and slammed it into the big man, pinning him against the wall. But Uziel was able to pull his knife from the scabbard he wore around his hips. Mace lifted the table off the floor and jammed it against the bigger man as Uziel stabbed with his blade. The tip of the knife poked through the tabletop, but Mace twisted the furniture, and the buried blade was pulled out of Uziel's hand.

Uziel's two companions tried to get to their feet, but Browneagle clubbed one from behind with his pistol barrel, and the man slumped to the floor. As the Indian Policeman leveled and cocked his pistol at the other man, that companion dropped back to his seat with his hands in the air.

The towering black man stepped out from where the table had pinned him against the wall to face Mace. With a grunt, Uziel broke off one of the upturned table legs and swung the club at the marshal's head. Mace sidestepped the blow, but jagged ends of the splintered wood raked his cheek and knocked off his hat. The killer cut the air with another blow. Mace put his head down and plowed into the man nailing him against the wall and pounding the breath out of him. Still, the big black man swung and hit Mace in the jaw with a staggering blow.

Mace was knocked back a step, and his whole face was both numb and pulsing with pain. Before Uziel could recover his wind, Mace took a step forward, grabbed Uziel by the front of his bib overalls, and jerked him forward. The marshal rocked down on his own back to the floor with a boot planted in the big man's middle. Then, when Uziel was help-less in midair, Mace let him drop to the floor -- landing on his head and leaving him stunned like a poleaxed mule.

They put the iron cuffs and chain on Uziel's hands behind

his muscled back. By the time he began to recover from the fight, still dazed, he was able to stand and walk on unsteady feet. Browneagle motioned his prisoners toward the door with his pistol.

Mace picked up his hat and wiped the blood from the scratches on his cheek.

"Why didn't you give me a hand?" he asked Browneagle.

"I did. But you wanted to know what the job was like."

The biggest whore house in Muskogee was Maude's "The Big House." Mace and Browneagle showed up there after getting Uziel and his two pards into Stoney's tumbleweed wagon. The lawmen waited in the entrance hall while the butler outfitted bouncer went to fetch the owner.

In the lounge behind them, scantily clad, made up, and openly available young women -- white, black, Indian, and oriental -- waited for business. Mace couldn't help but look while Browneagle kept his back to the room.

Big Maude wore a red dress that exposed her arms, back, and all the cleavage she could from between her enormous breasts. A brown wart beside her left eye drew everyone's attention away from her large hooked nose. It was more dominate even than the pipe she smoked.

"You boys interested in something besides what's on the buffet?"

Mace opened his vest, and Browneagle turned to display their badges.

"I don't give different prices for anyone," Big Maude's smile and her voice changed from friendly to hostile.

"We're looking for information about Bart Zolan."

"You going to shoot that son-of-a-bitch?"

"We plan to arrest him and take him back to Ft. Smith to stand trial for murder."

The madame thought a moment before she spoke again.

"I'd rather see him shot full of holes -- but if that's the best you can do -- I'll go to Arkansas to testify against the bastard."

"Did you witness the murder?"

"No. But I knew he was with Tollie. And after he killed her and crawled out the window --," she used the stem of her pipe to push open Mace's vest and tapped his badge, " -- I'm the one who discovered his badge after he got away."

"That will do," Mace said. "Do you have any idea where we might find him?"

"I hear he's out in Burns Flat. Cheyenne-Arapaho country. If that's where the little weasel is, it won't be hard to find him."

"We'll take a look," Mace said. "And are you serious about testifying against him?"

"Honey, you can bet my tits on that. And that's a hell of a bet."

CHAPTER 16

The first hanging that took place for Judge Parker's court was a double hanging. Handsome murderer and rapist Baxter Field took the thirteen steps up to the gallows ahead of Avery Sinil. Sinil was a braggart, a drunk and back shooter, as well as a Kiowa warrior whose father had married a black slave woman he owned. Although not on trial for that murder, his mother was Sinil's first killing. He regretted his life and took it out joyfully on anyone who he deemed weaker than him.

There being no official hangman, the job fell to jailer Herb Irwin.

As the newspaper both described the executions, they were "ghastly." Not having tied the nooses properly, both men dangled at the end of their ropes and kicked and squirmed until they choked to death.

Claxton Landers had called it "brutal yet savage justice" in his Ft. Smith Daily Ledger. Joseph Pickering's Vindicator celebrated the torturous scene as "justifiable compensation" for "the barbarous lawbreakers."

Hundreds of onlookers who had gathered in almost a

picnic fashion to view the event were sickened by what they had witnessed. Still, no one doubted that justice had been done and that both men deserved to die horribly.

As would be his practice, Judge Parker was not in attendance for the executions. Instead, he always took the day off and was nowhere near the gallows when the condemned met their fate.

Judge Parker's wife, Mary O'Tool Parker, and their two children, 5-year-old James and 7-year-old Charles, arrived by steamboat in Ft. Smith at the end of his first month on the bench -- only a couple of days after the executions. The family took possession of the old two-story stone commissary building for their home.

First Charles and a year later, James, attended the local public school, and the Parkers joined the Methodist church. The judge made it a habit to walk the six blocks to court six days a week, getting to know the people of the town and making sure his family members were involved in the community.

The people of Ft. Smith began to have faith and hope in the new judge and his court despite the spectacles of the dual executions. Yet, lawlessness was still the rule across the river in the Indian Territory. For this to change, the Marshal's Service would have to bring significant fugitives to face the court's justice.

The judge continued his six days a week schedule of holding court from nine in the morning until sunset. Over the course of the first two months, he had seen each interested attorney, practice in front of his bench. He made his decision about recommending a court prosecutor and summoned Temple Houston to his office.

Temple Houston arrived half past noon as Judge Parker was finishing his lunch. Clerk Presley Cross showed the lawyer into the Judge's chambers. The jurist rose and shook hands with the white-clad visitor and offered him a seat.

"Oh, Mr. Cross," the judge called as the clerk was about to leave. "We need a bailiff. Do you have any suggestions?"

"Ah -- none spring to mind immediately, Your Honor."

"If I may," Temple offered. "Former Sheriff Hershel Adrian isn't finding the restaurant business as appealing or as profitable as he expected. He's a man who can handle himself and might be very interested."

"Mr. Cross?" the judge asked.

"Well, Sheriff Adrian was considered a fair man and was respected. He didn't run for re-election after he had been shot in the leg by a drunk he was trying to arrest."

"If he left the restaurant business alone," Temple added, "and let his two daughters run it, I bet it would do better than it is with Hershel in charge. He's not a businessman."

"Would you speak to him, Mr. Cross? I want to visit with him."

"Yes, Your Honor."

With that, the clerk left, and Temple took a chair across from Judge Parker, who took his seat behind his desk.

"I'll not beat about the bush, Mr. Houston," he began. "I've decided to recommend Rupert Dalby for the position of District Attorney."

"I see," Temple said, showing no emotion.

"The reason I'm telling you first is that you are clearly a better attorney than anyone in town and the logical choice for the position -- which you may apply for on your own if you choose. This appointment comes through the newly established Department of Justice and will be made by the President. I know you have the political connections to make a good case for your appointment -- and if you were appointed, I have no doubt you would be a fine prosecutor."

"But there's something more, isn't there?" Your Honor.

"The simple truth, Mr. Houston, is that I do not need your help to put men in prison or even to sentence them to death if their crimes deserve it. But for justice to be served, the accused will always need a strong, impassioned, clever, and witty attorney to speak for them. We both know that is not Rupert Dalby -- nor many of the other attorneys currently practicing in Ft. Smith."

The judge let these words sink in before he went on.

"What I'm saying is that I -- that justice -- needs you on the other side of the courtroom. I don't mean to insult you in any way, Mr. Houston -- having seen your work, I am much impressed with your legal mind."

"Your Honor, I am not insulted. I know you could have had a better paying and more prestigious position as Chief Justice of the Utah Territory. But you requested this job -- I believe because of your sense of law and order -- and justice. I consider this to be a -- somewhat -- backhanded compliment -- and I accept your decision. I will not try to go over or around you, Sir."

Temple Houston got to his feet and extended his hand to the judge.

"Thank you for telling me, Your Honor, and for your consideration." The lawyer bowed his head slightly, saying, "I am your servant, Sir."

CHAPTER 17

Burns Flat was five days ride through the Territory and almost catty-corner to Muskogee. The town had only seven buildings, and three of them were mostly tents. One of the predominately canvas structures had a sign out front which read, "Stick and Balls."

Mace Truax and John Browneagle tied up their horses out front late one afternoon and went inside. Several games were going on at three different tables, and there was a bar. Mace and Browneagle took places at an empty table. The Indian Policeman had his badge in his pocket. A barkeep brought empty coffee cups and a pot.

"What can I get for ya'?"

"Coffee'll do for now."

The barkeep poured each man's tin cup full.

"What's your specialty," Mace asked.

"Pool -- 5 cents a game -- and root beer."

"We'll stick with coffee," Mace said, tossing some coins on the table. "And we'll play a game when there's an open table.

The mostly bald barkeep scraped up the coins and returned to the bar.

Mace and Browneagle sipped their coffee, examining the bar.

There was a card game going on towards the rear. One of the men looked like the description of Bart Zolan -- overweight, mid-'40s, hairy lump of a man. He hadn't shaved in almost a week. His weak chin and yellow teeth were his main facial features.

There were three other men at the table, one was a ranch hand in tired old boots, and a bushy head of dark hair. Another was a drummer in a wrinkled tweed suit with a dusty bowler hat. The dealer was a slick-looking younger man with blonde hair, a flat-brimmed hat, and a thin cigar hanging out of one side of his mouth.

Mace and Browneagle took over a pool table near the card table and knocked the balls around without really trying to play. As they were going through the motions, it happened again. Out of nowhere, for no reason, Mace discovered his mind had flashed on the image of Delta Wadsworth.

"Shit!" the cowboy said, throwing down his hand after being dealt three cards. "I'm done." He stood.

"You'll get paid next month," the dealer said with a nasty grin. "Come back then, and we'll teach you some more."

The cowboy scuffed his heels on the dirt floor as he pulled down his hat and pushed his way out the tent flap.

The dealer raked in the winnings from the center of the table. Mace put up his pool cue and stepped over to the table.

"Mind if I sit in?" Mace asked.

"We're glad t' take your money as much as anyone else, stranger," the dealer said.

Several hands were played, and Mace won one hand.

"We've got a sharp one here, Bart," the dealer said to the overweight man beside him.

"Let's see how long his luck holds."

The deal passed to Bart Zolan. The drummer cut the cards, and Bart dealt.

The pot slowly grew, and finally, the drummer folded and stood up.

"You boys are getting too rich for me," he said, stepping away from the table and going to the bar.

"Got a name, stranger?" the slick player asked as Mace raised again.

"Yep," was all Mace said.

"This here is "Waco" Bill Lamar," Zolan said.

"I've killed me a Texas sheriff 'for I came to the territory," the younger man bragged. "Knocked on his front door at supper. He left his wife at the table and still had a napkin tucked in his shirt as he pulled open the door. I told him who I was -- and then I shot him right through the napkin."

"Waco's not a man t' mess with," Zolan said as Waco raised again. Zolan added a greenback to the pot. Mace sat there, studying the two men.

"Either raise or call," the pistolero said.

Mace looked down at his cards again and then reached inside his vest and removed his badge, tossing it onto of the pile face down.

"What's that?" Zolan asked, reaching out and flipping the six-pointed star over. He paused and swallowed as he read, "U.S. Marshal. This was my badge," Zolan said slowly.

Mace laid a folded piece of paper across the badge. "And this is a warrant for your arrest, Bart Zolan. The charge is the murder of Tollie Fredricks."

Bart eased his chair back and got ready to go for his gun as the drummer dropped to the ground, trying to cover his head with his hands at the bar.

"Hold it, Bart," the young gunfighter beside him said, getting to his feet. "I never had a chance t' take on a U.S. Marshal. I want to do this one."

Mace rose, too, as Browneagle laid his stick on the table nearby and casually stepped up behind Zolan.

The confident shootist flipped his cigar to the dirt with his right hand as he reached around behind his back and pulled his duster away from the pistol that hung off his right hip.

Zolan felt a pistol barrel against his spine and froze.

Mace's palm was almost touching the butt of his Remington when he saw a slight turn in Waco's left arm as the man pulled his duster behind his back. Mace suddenly drew and shot Waco Bill Lamar in the heart. The young gunman had a startled look on his face as his knees gave out and he dropped back to his chair and then to the floor.

Before Bart Zolan could move, the audible click of the hammer on Browneagle's pistol was heard.

"You killed him in cold blood," the barkeep said, pulling up a shotgun from behind the bar. "Marshal or not, that's murder."

"Roll him over," Mace said, still holding his smoking revolver level with where Lamar had stood.

The barkeep stepped around the planks of the bar with his shortened double barrel. He kept the weapon aimed at Mace as he stepped over the dead gunman. Stooping, the barkeep pulled the body over. The left hand flopped out, and a short pistol dropped from his fingers.

The barkeep lowered his shotgun and looked up at Mace.

"How'd you know?"

"It's part of the job," he said, holstering his gun and reaching for the warrant and his badge on the table.

Browneagle had Bart Zolan's six-shooter.

"We've got some bracelets just your size," Mace said to Bart Zolan. "And a long tumbleweed ride back to Ft. Smith."

"What about him?" the barkeep asked, indicating Waco.

Mace leaned over and unbuckled the dead shootist's gun

belt and pulled it free. He collected both pistols and examined the belt before he reached down and picked up the flat-brimmed hat on the ground beside the body. Inside the hatband, the name "Waco Bill Lamar" was burned into the leather.

From the money on the table, he pulled out two twenty-dollar gold pieces. Mace stacked them together and handed them to the barkeep.

"You can keep the change," Mace said.

CHAPTER 18

The Overland Stagecoach was bouncing east along the Deep Fork of the Canadian River. The driver, a former buffalo hunter named Atlas Ayars, applied the brakes as the wooden conveyance topped a rise and started down toward the slow running stream. He allowed the six horses to stop and drink before starting up once more. The stage had just cleared the water when bandits struck.

Atlas pulled up on the reins and brought everything to a rattling stop. He knew he could have run over the neckerchief face covered man in the road, but when two more gunmen stepped out, one on each side, the driver didn't see the point. He knew he wasn't carrying a payroll or bank deposit and had only two passengers, a middle-aged couple. These boys with the guns were going to be disappointed at their haul. But nobody needed to get shot -- so he stopped and raised his hands.

"Get down!" the tough-sounding bandit to the driver's left shouted.

Atlas wrapped the reins around the brake handle and

climbed down, keeping his hands up and offering no resistance. It wasn't the first time he'd been robbed, and he didn't figure it would be the last.

The paper-thin robber, who had been the first to step out in the road, moved around with his long double-barreled shotgun to join the one who seemed like the leader holding a Colt revolver.

"I got no strongbox," Atlas said as the shotgun carrying thief came up past the horses to cover the driver.

"Shut up!" the leader told the driver. As soon as the first man leveled his .12 gauge, the leader stepped over and yanked open the stage door.

"Get out!" he yelled at the passengers, "-- and don't you try nothin'!"

The man, in his early 50's, stepped down first then offered his hand to his wife only a year or two younger than him. He wore a three-piece suit with a gold chain across his flat belly from vest pocket to vest pocket. He had a full head of gray-streaked hair. His wife, in a full dress and jacket, her graying streaked hair under a bonnet, said not a word.

The couple was Watt and Inola Grayson -- full-blooded Creek Indians who had seen the future and adopted the white man's ways. Their ranch on the Deep Fork and his investments in the lumber and other businesses had made them wealthy -- even though they neither dressed nor acted like it.

The third bandit came around the back of the wagon once the couple had climbed down. This one caught the watch and chain their leader snatched from the passenger's vest.

Atlas looked over at the couple and didn't see the thin bandit raise his weapon before he crashed it into the driver's head, knocking him to the ground.

"Tie him to the wheel," the leader demanded.

The first man leaned his shotgun against a large rock and brought out two leather strips with which he bound the man to the front wheel. Watt made no sound, but his wife had to bite her lip as she saw her husband shoved to the ground and his wrists tightly secured to the rim of the wheel. The third robber held a pistol to the woman's side, so she kept her hands raised.

Without any warning, the leader smashed his pistol against Watt's chin -- first on one side and then the other.

Inola closed her eyes a moment but made no sound.

"This is the way it's going to be -- again and again -- until you tell me where you keep your gold, Grayson!" the leader snarled. It was clear he knew who the couple was and they were the reason for the robbery.

Watt spat blood and a tooth but said nothing. The leader hit him again and kicked him in the stomach. When Watt didn't respond, the head bandit holstered his pistol and went to work with his fists battering the older man mercilessly.

The thin man retrieved his shotgun and slammed the butt of the weapon into the victims' shins and legs. A clear crack of bone was heard. Still, Watt said nothing.

"This is taking too long," the third bandit said. This was clearly a woman. She yanked down her bandanna as the leader continued to batter the helpless man tied to the wheel.

When the two men got winded from delivering the beating, they pulled down their masks. The leader seemed to notice the wife for the first time and stepped over and grabbed her. Using his gloved hands, he slapped her face knocking her to the ground. But Inola, too, was silent.

"Then we might as well have a little fun," the leader gasps between breaths. He pulled the woman to her feet and dragged her to a boulder and threw her face down across it. The man, Watt, now recognized as Emmitt Buckholde, a loudmouth, a bully, and known card cheat, ripped Inola's dress apart at its back seams exposing her flesh. He lifted her dress from the ground and pulled the fabric apart from hem to waist.

"No!" Watt called through his bloody mouth.

The thin man got down on his knees at eye level with Watt.

"By God, I think he's goin' t' talk!"

Watt glanced at Doc Kellen, a former Union war medic turned outlaw. He looked up at the armed woman and knew she was Bell Starr.

Emmitt Buckholde returned and stood over Watt.

"Tell us or I swear to God I'll rape and kill her!"

Watt took a breath and was able to only mumble through swollen and bloody lips, "In the well -- behind the house. A loose --," he swallowed, "a loose brick on the side -- closest to the house."

"How much?" Buckholde demanded!

Watt breathed hard, so Buckholde pulled his pistol and stepped back over to the prostrate figure of Watt's wife. Buckholde cocked his pistol.

"Tell me!" he shouted.

"Thirty -- thousand."

"Gold?"

Watt managed to nod his head.

Buckholde fired his pistol into Inola's spine.

Then he turned and shot Watt three times before shooting Atlas once in the head.

Bell said, "You better hope he wasn't lyin'!"

"He wasn't," Buckholde said confidently.

"We'll never be able to ask him again now."

"Did you think we were going to take him -- or her -- along with us?"

Neither of the other two bandits answered.

"I didn't think so either. Cut the horses loose -- no point in letting them become buzzard meat still in the harness. By the time they make it to the next stop, we'll be long gone."

And they were.

CHAPTER 19

As Mace and Browneagle led Stoney and the prison wagon across the Indian Territory towards Ft. Smith, Judge Parker continued to hold court and dispense justice.

"If Your Excellency will let me," a fuzzy-headed Irishman said, standing at the defense table as the new bailiff, retired sheriff, Hershel Adrian, called the case of Cormac O'Rourke, "I'd like to plead me own case."

"It's *Your Honor,*" his appointed attorney, Temple Houston, leaned forward from his seat speaking to his client.

"Beggin' your pardon -- Your Honor."

"Mr. O'Rourke," Judge Parker said, looking at the well-worn and patched coat and pants the man who stood was wearing, "the court-appointed you an attorney -- a good one -- I might add, so that you will be properly represented. The finer points of the law are not always easily known nor understood."

"I thank Your Honor, and I thank Mr. Houston, but," the ginger hair and medium bearded man said, "I can speak for meself."

"As you wish, Mr. O'Rourke. How do you plead to the charges of operating an illegal distillery."

"Guilty," O'Rourke said without any hesitation.

"Are you sure?" the judge asked.

"I've been a whiskey maker for seventeen-year, Your Honor. Before the famine drove me family and me from County Cork, I was known as a master of me craft."

"Do you understand that to -- practice your craft here you need a license and are required to pay taxes on your product?"

"Aware I am, Your Honor. Willing, I am not. I'll do prison time, but I'll not finance the lords and ladies and their fancy houses and carriages while my family barely gets by."

"There are no lord or titled ladies in this country, Mr. O'Rourke."

The accused stood mute.

The judge tried another tact.

"Your children, Mr. O'Rourke, do they attend school?"

"They do. I'm hopin' they'll be educated and have a better life than ever I've been able to provide."

"The license fee and the revenue taxes on your product, Mr. O'Rourke, they go to build our schools, pay our teachers -- build and maintain our roads. The taxes required are not from some government or royal decree -- they are laws and rates set by you and your neighbor's representatives. In other words, we, you and I, decide what the fees and taxes are and what they will be used for."

The pale blue eyes of the defendant darted back and forth as he processed what the judge had said.

"You have the right to object and argue against the rates if you believe them to be unfair. This is the American way, Mr. O'Rourke."

"Your Honor must think me dumb as an ox, but I'd never thought of it that way. It has been me and me family's tradition to avoid the revenuers and all such taxes. I can see now there is more to it than I ever considered."

"Do you still stand by your plea?"

Standing up straight, O'Rourke said, "I do, Your Honor. I am an honest man -- and what I have done is indeed a crime. I am guilty."

There was a murmur in the court before Judge Parker spoke once again.

"I sentence you to two years in prison, Cormac O'Rourke -- but I will suspend the sentence if you agree to abide by the law as you practice your craft in the future."

The Irishman was amazed at the words he heard.

"Do you mean I will not go to prison?"

"If you agree to set up a legal distillery and pay all legally applicable fees and taxes."

"A legal distillery. I've never done that." O'Rourke let out a breath and bowed his head. "It is a noble thing you are offering me, Your Honor, to be sure -- but I have no money to begin such a business. Truly good Irish whiskey will need to be aged -- three to seven years -- maybe more. I thank Your Honor -- but I don't see how I could possibly do this. I am able to do the prison time, and somehow my family will have to survive without me."

"Then," Judge Parker said with a sigh, "will the bailiff take Mr. O'Rourke into custody."

Hershel Adrian stepped toward the defendant. Adrian was a solidly built man who, in middle age, was not going to fat. He had about him a look of strength and solidity.

"If I may, Your Honor," Temple Houston said getting to his feet, "-- it might very well be possible -- indeed even prob- able -- that investment funds could be found to establish such an enterprise -- and fund it until such time as it can begin to turn a profit."

Cormac O'Rourke was stunned as he looked over his shoulder at his attorney.

"A truly good Irish whiskey would be much in demand," Houston continued, "-- and I will pledge to be the first investor."

"Mr. O'Rourke," the judge said, "it is up to you."

"Well, I never," O'Rourke said. "Your Honor, I will accept your terms -- and Mr. Houston's support. I would be pleased to become an honest and legal businessman in this great country."

The prison wagon was about half full. The tumbleweed entourage with four horses pulling, the whiskey wagon trailing behind, plus two other horses, was about to cross out of Seminole country and was headed into Creek - Cherokee land. Three armed riders rushed out of the brush, one from each side and one dead ahead. The front rider grabbed the reins of the lead horse on the left, a second did the same to the second pair also from the left when their leader pulled up near Stoney from the right. His revolver was pointed at the one-legged driver.

"Whoa up there!" Stoney called, pulling back on the reins and bringing the whole procession to a halt. Dropping the reins, Stoney lifted both his hands above his head under the lip of the tumbleweed wagon's overhang.

"What have the heavens delivered into our hands?" the rider nearest Stoney said. His name was Rosco, and he fancied himself a circuit-riding preacher on a mission from the devil.

"I'm a deputy U.S. Marshal," Stoney said, raising his hands until his fingers were out of sight in the overhang. "I'm taking these men to Ft. Smith to stand trial."

"Are you now?" the leader laughed. He kept his pistol trained on Stoney but urged his horse back a couple of paces so he could see the men in the cage. "I don't expect you're carrying any cash to feed these unfortunate men with are you?"

"I do their cookin'," Stoney said, his fingers locating his hidden shotgun.

"And what's in the back wagon there?"

"Evidence," Stoney said.

"There are two more of them!" Bart Zolan called out from between the bars."

"Are there?" Rocco asked, looking around as Browneagle stepped into the road ahead of the first rider, his Winchester leveled at the man holding the front pair of horses.

Mace rode up from the rear his Henry leveled at the second man. The second man released the reins he held and threw up his hands.

When Rosco turned back, Stoney had his shortened double-barrel aimed dead center of the man even though his revolver remained trained on the driver.

"Drop your guns," Mace said. "All of you."

"And what if I choose not to?" Rocco asked, cocking his pistol.

"You might hit Stoney," Mace said, "-- could even kill him -- but you'd be dead and on your way to hell before you ever knew for sure."

"They got us, Rosco," the second man said, unbuckling his gun belt and letting it fall to the ground.

The man at the front could tell by the look in Browneagle's eyes that there was no hesitation in this Indian. He, too, took off his holster and belt and carefully eased it to the ground.

"Looks as if I've got nothing to lose," Rosco said. "I ain't about to go be hung. I hear they can't even do that right in Ft. Smith."

"At least in court, you have a chance," Mace told him. "Stoney, doesn't miss."

"I've already lost a leg," Stoney said propping this peg leg up on the wagon's toe board

For several moments there was silence as the standoff continued.

"Ask yourself this," Stoney said. "Have you had all the pussy you ever want? You pull that trigger, and I guran-damn-tee you'll never get any more."

"And I won't get any if they hang me, either."

"*If --*," Mace emphasized. "Otherwise, you got *no* chance."

For whatever reason, Rosco released his grip, and his pistol dropped to the dirt.

CHAPTER 20

The man laying in the Tulsey Town hospital didn't look a thing like Watt Grayson, wealthy Creek Indian. In his late 50s with a full head of gray-streaked hair, the man was bandaged from navel to armpit -- every finger splinted, and his head wrapped in a gauze mask. The skin that could be seen was dark purple, blue, and swollen. The patient slowly pried open his eyelids and forced himself to speak through battered and puffy lips.

"John Browneagle," he made himself say and then licked his cracked lips.

Mace poured a glass of water from the pitcher on the bedside table and helped the man sip until he was able to nod his head.

"Who -- are -- you?" he asked.

"Mace Truax. I'm the new U.S. Marshal from Ft. Smith."

"No -- offense -- but I -- don't -- know you. I -- trust -- John -- Browneagle."

"No offense taken," Mace said, stepping aside so his Choctaw companion could get closer to the bed."

"You can trust him, Mr. Grayson," Browneagle said.

Mace didn't expect to ever hear those words from the Indian Policeman.

The injured man slowly turned his head and looked at Mace.

"Thank -- you -- for -- coming."

"We were taking a wagon load of prisoners to Ft. Smith," Browneagle said. "Sheriff Linbocker caught up with us after we passed through town. He told us what had happened to you and Inola. Said it was out of his jurisdiction. It is in ours."

The man sagged in his bed and was able to nod his head and closed his eyes.

Browneagle went on, "They must have thought you were dead or they wouldn't have left you. Do you know who they were?"

Watt Grayson breathed a few times, opened his eyes once more before he began making the effort it would take to answer this question.

"Emmitt -- Buck -- holde -- Doc -- Kellen -- and -- Bell Starr."

"Did they all take part in the shooting?"

Grayson moved his head from side to side. Then he said, "Only -- Buck -- holde."

"I promise you they will all stand trial -- and pay for this."

Before he could say anything else, the patient closed his eyes and seemed to go to sleep.

"Let him sleep," the doctor said. "You have lifted a great burden from his shoulders. Do you think you can really catch these three?"

"I gave my word," Browneagle said as if that was enough to answer the question definitively.

Outside the hospital and back in the saddle, Mace asked, "I would have never guessed you could talk so much."

"When there's a need."

Mace said, "Even I've heard about Bell Starr's hideout. After we deliver this bunch, I will be willing to go with you."

"They know me," Browneagle said. "By now, they will have even heard of you. There is only one man who can do this. I'll take you to him."

They rode out of town and soon rejoined Stoney and the tumbleweed caravan.

As they rode, there it was again. The image of that young widow. They had not spoken but for even half an hour -- and here he was thinking about her once more. That had to mean something.

Knut Marble, known to all as "Big Indian," was a powerful man who towered over both his attorneys, even sitting at the defense table. He was charged with the murder of his white wife, who had served him something he didn't like for dinner. There were stories about this feared Kiowa that he had murdered others, but no one would testify against him.

Completely stoic, the man said not a word since he found himself behind bars in a marshal's tumbleweed wagon, chained up like a prize hog. He had been dead drunk when he was taken into custody.

There had been no doubt about his guilt nor the results of the trial, but some companions had produced enough, most likely stolen, money to purchase the services of two of Ft. Smith's better lawyers, pear-shaped attorney Brice Nuese and hunchbacked Lon Kearney.

Rupert Dalby wasn't officially the District Attorney, but all the recommendations had been made, and everyone knew it was simply a matter of time before the official appointment. In the interim, the other lawyers interested in the position had yielded to the inevitable and stepped aside. Dalby was the unofficial prosecutor.

In the gallery, the editors of both papers, squat 50's Claxton Landers of the *Daily Ledger* and Pick Pickering of *The Vindicator*, wire-rimmed glasses and balding with his bowler hat in his lap, were taking notes. This trial was the biggest story in town.

It was a sweltering day in July, and all the court's windows were open in the hope of attracting any hint of a breeze. After an older woman had finished testifying against Knut Marble -- she is the one who discovered the wife's hacked-up body -- the bailiff, Hershel Adrian, helped the lady down from the witness box beside the judge's desk close to the jury.

At that same moment, both of Big Indian's lawyers were discussing a point of law with Rupert Dalby. This was the instant when the defendant jerked to his feet, bounded upon the defense table, and leaped across to Judge Parker's desk. He turned and readied himself for a dive out the window near the judge's bench when Judge Parker spun and managed to grab the attempting escapee around both legs. Big Indian was already in the air when the judge became attached, and the two bodies crashed to the floor just short of the window.

In an instant, Hershel Adrian was there and knew right were to club the large man behind his ear with the pistol the Bailiff carried -- since Temple Houston's stunt during Stoney's trial, this was the only weapon allowed in the court. Big Indian was slamming his handcuffed fists against the judge in hopes of dislodging his impediment. But the bailiff's years as sheriff had taught him exactly where to strike. In the space of a single breath, the huge man went limp.

It took Adrian and both of Big Indian's attorneys to lug the man's body back to his chair. Leg cuffs and other chains were used to secure the man to his seat. By the time he came around, Knut Marble discovered himself immobilized, and his trial was continuing.

In the end, he was sentenced to death by hanging.

Stoney Welch filled one raft with both wagons and his horses when their troupe reached the Arkansas River. Mace and Browneagle helped load and reconnect the tumbleweed train before they rode on North as Stoney headed for Ft. Smith.

The two-story house they reached mid-afternoon was plain but appeared well constructed. Three black children were playing in the yard as the two riders approached. When the little ones became aware of the travelers, they bolted for the house. Mace and Browneagle pulled up at the edge of a rail fence.

"Hello, the house!" Browneagle called.

It was a full minute before the front door opened a crack, and a Winchester protruded from the shadows in the house.

"John Browneagle," the voice called from inside, "I recognize you. Who's that with you?"

"The new marshal. Mace Truax."

The rifle was lowered, and a tall black man with a bushy mustache stepped out, holding the weapon down by his leg.

"Come ahead on."

Browneagle led the way, and Mace pulled up beside him.

"Bass Reeves," Browneagle said, "I wanted you to meet Marshal Truax. We captured the old marshal, Bart Zolan, and he's on his way to Ft. Smith."

"Marshal," the man said in a welcoming tone. Step down both of you. What can I do for you?"

Both riders looped their reins to the single-pole hitching post.

"You know Watt and Iona Grayson?"

"Heard of them. Nice couple, they say. Creek. Done real well for himself."

"They were on a stage that was held up. Mrs. Grayson and the driver were killed. They left Watt for dead."

"Not too smart. I hear he's a tough ol' bird -- even in his younger years. Who did it?"

"Emmitt Buckholde was the shooter. Bell Starr and Doc Kellen were the other two."

"So they're likely hold up at Younger Bend."

"That's what I think."

"The marshal agrees with you?"

"I'm new to the territory -- just out of the army. I'm learning. But it looks that way to me from what I know."

Reeves's wife brought out a pitcher and some glasses for lemonade.

"Thank you, ma'am," Mace tipped his hat.

Browneagle nodded his head and said, "Jennie."

She was a small woman compared to her 6 foot 2 inch, 180-pound husband. But the way she carried herself was with strength and purpose.

Back inside, she shooed their children back outside.

"Play outside," she said to them. "I don't want you under my feet."

Bass Reeves eased the hammer down on his rifle and motioned for Browneagle and Mace to follow him to a bench and a stump under the shade of a pecan tree. The black man took a seat on the board of a swing suspended by looped rope from a thick branch.

"I heard there was a new judge."

"There is," Browneagle said.

"Word is he's not like any of those judges before him."

"We've been on a scout," Browneagle said, "but we hear the same things."

Reeves nodded his head.

"Can you tell Marshal Truax a little about yourself, Bass?" Browneagle asked.

Shrugging his shoulder, Reeves said, "I was born and grew up a slave. During the war, I was taken up to the Territory to help fight for the South. I escaped. Since the war, I've lived among several of the tribes."

"You speak, Choctaw, Cherokee, Creek, Seminole -- and some Apache." Browneagle offered.

"It helped if I was goin' to live there."

"You've worked as a guide for some deputies out of Van Buren when the court was there," Browneagle said.

"I have. You interested in me for that again?"

"John Browneagle tells me I should be looking at you as a new Deputy Marshal, Mr. Reeves."

Bass was more than a little surprised at this statement.

"A man like yourself," Mace continued, "who knows the land -- can speak to some of the tribes -- in their native tongue -- and I understand you can handle yourself and firearms well."

The black man leaned over and rested his Winchester on the ground and against the base of the tree. When he met Mace's eyes, he said apologetically, "I can't read, Marshal."

Mace looked at Browneagle, who said, "He can read a trail as good as me -- read men better."

"But there would be paper to read and sign," the black man said.

CHAPTER 21

Stoney's collection of prisoners had already been unloaded and lodged in the jail by the time Mace and Browneagle returned to Ft. Smith. Mace stepped down from his saddle at the livery.

"Thank you, John Browneagle, for going with me," Mace said extending a hand to his partner, " -- and --." he added rubbing his jaw where the bruising was almost gone from his fight with the black killer, Uziel, "-- for showing me the way it is."

"I wish you would call me John."

Mace wasn't expecting this as they shook hands. It took him a moment before he smiled and said. "I would be honored. And please do me a favor, and let's make it, Mace."

"I will swear out the warrants for Buckholde and the other with Mr. Cross," Browneagle told Mace, " -- then you know where I camp. When I am needed to testify, send word. I will come."

John Browneagle turned and rode toward the courthouse.

The muscular young farrier, Buster Pettijohn, approached Mace from inside the livery.

"Marshal," the young stableman greeted Mace taking the lawman's horse.

Mace patted his mount on the neck. "She's been very reliable like you said, Buster," he told the aproned young man. "Please see she gets extra oats and a good rubdown."

"That I will," the smith said, leading Mace's horse inside.

Mace was in no hurry to go up to his office. After a month on the trail, he thought a drink was in order and so headed for the Sidewheeler. He wanted to stop by the mercantile but knew he didn't have a good reason -- especially until he got a bath, a shave and a haircut. But as he passed the general store, he noticed a sign in the window which hadn't been there the only other time he'd visited the establishment. The sign read: "Rooms To Rent."

"Marshal," the clean-shaven proprietor, wearing his wire-rimmed spectacles on the top of his thinning gray hair, greeted Mace as he entered. "Glad to see you back."

"Mr. Keeling," Mace said, trying not to be obvious as he scanned the place for the man's daughter.

"How can we help you today?"

"I saw the sign in the window -- about rooms for rent?"

"Yes, indeed," the jolly owner said. "The whole upstairs," he waved a hand toward the ceiling.

"Oh," Mace said, trying to keep the disappointment from his voice.

"More than you're looking for?"

"I believe all I need is a place t' hang my hat."

"If you decide to stay in Ft. Smith, Marshal, you could decide you wanted a little more space."

Just then, she entered from the back of the store, carrying an armful of fabric bolts. Delta Keeling Wadsworth was everything Mace had remembered, winsome, delicate but steady, striking without being overpowering.

Not one to miss anything, her father turned and called to his daughter.

"Delta."

She looked up, put down her load, and crossed to the two men brushing back a nonexistent stray strand of hair.

"Marshal. We've been wondering how you were doing out on -- patrol or whatever you call it."

"Scouting," he said, taking off his dusty hat.

"Marshal Truax noticed our room for rent sign in the window. He's afraid it's more than he would want. Perhaps you could show it to him."

"Of course," she said with a genuine smile that reached the deep brown pools of her lovely eyes. "Let me get the keys."

Mace watched her walk away -- paying more attention to her figure than he knew he had any right to.

"You know, Marshal," Mr. Keeling said, scratching his head, "it would be a good thing for us to have a lawman living above the store. We could give you a very reasonable rent."

"Uh-huh," Mace said, trying to pull his attention back to the proprietor.

"This way, Marshal," Delta said after she had taken a set of keys from the cash register.

He followed her to the rear of the store, where a closed and locked door opened on a staircase to the second floor. He followed her entranced by the movements of her body. She stopped at the landing and unlocked another door on her right. She stepped inside, and he followed.

"The kitchen with a new stove," she pointed out the first room. "I don't know how much of your own cooking you do, Marshal."

"Not much at all," he said.

"Well, at least you can prepare your coffee."

She turned around to another door, slipped the key into

the lock, and twisted it. She pulled it open and gestured outside.

"There is also an outside entrance," she said. "The stairs lead down to the street. No need to have to come to the store every time," she said. What she didn't know was that wasn't a selling point to the lawman. Why would he not want to come through the store even if he only caught a glimpse of her?

She closed the door and walked into the next room. There was a fireplace at the far end. Beside the fireplace was a window. Another window was behind them looking out over the stairs.

Delta moved on and showed him the bedroom where a bed frame with no mattress stood. A potbellied stove stood in one corner. There were a washbowl and pitcher on a table, a new slop jar beside the bed, and a pair of double windows facing the street.

"This is more room than I've ever had."

"Even as an officer?" she asked.

How did she know about his service?

"The posts where I was assigned," he said, "were rather primitive -- even the best of them."

It suddenly hit him what was different about her. She was no longer wearing black. It must have been over a year now since her young husband was killed.

"As the U.S. Marshal, you should have a nice place. You're going to be an important member of the community."

"I haven't thought about that."

"You might like it here -- even put down some roots. Get married and start a family."

"That's --," he didn't know how to finish that thought.

They stood looking at each other for a long moment. She began to blush.

"Marshal, like Papa, said, we'd be very proud to have you

living here. I could help you find some furniture -- it could be just what you need."

"Yeah," Mace said, unable to look away.

"You want to think about it?"

He didn't know how long he waited and just breathed. Finally, he nodded his head. "I'll take it."

She held out the keys to him and offered him her hand. He took it, and they shook -- although what Mace felt was only her warmth and the tenderness of her small hand in his.

"I'm also going to need to find a house," Mace said.

"A house?"

"For my widowed sister and her family."

"I think father will be the one to ask about that."

Mace left his gear in his new rooms and took the outside door and stairs to the street. He located a barber, got a bath, a haircut, and a shave before he changed into a clean shirt and pants. The barber told him to leave what he needed to be washed, and he'd see his clothes were taken care of.

The sun was setting, and Stoney Welch was slouched back at a table right inside the door of the Sidewheeler when Mace entered. Mace got a beer from Jules at the bar and joined his deputy at the table.

"You got yourself all prettied up for somebody, Marshal?"

"Myself."

Stoney laughed. The idea of bathing for yourself was something he didn't get.

"This here's a nice place," Stony observed. "But I never thought I'd be back in here."

"Why?"

"This is where I shot Tom Bartlett for cheatin' at cards. There was a big stink about who drew first. 'Course I knew

Bartlett did -- but even ol' Jules over there wasn't too sure. There was almost a lynch mob in here that night before I got out. I thought fer sure Jules thought I pulled first. But since the trial -- well ever'thin' been dandy. Even Jules treats me like I'm somebody."

"You are somebody, Stoney. You're a U.S. Deputy Marshal."

"Court must be over," Stoney said, nodding toward Presley Cross, the short, thin court clerk who pushed the batwing doors open. He walked straight to the bar but had to wait a few moments until Jules noticed him among the ever-growing evening crowd. Even the second bartender was busy with customers.

"Mr. Cross. What can I do for you?" Jules finally asked.

"It's not for me. Judge Parker asked if I could see about reserving your backroom for tomorrow night."

"I think we're clear," the barkeep said. "Why don't you check the calendar on my desk back there?" Jules motioned to the office door at the far end of the bar.

Cross craned his neck and then went where he was directed. The barkeep got back to his customers.

"To new jobs," Stoney said, lifting his glass.

"You've decided to stay on as a Deputy?" Mace asked.

"Yep. But it's not like you think, Marshal."

"How's that? You want to serve warrants yourself."

"In a way. See I got me a new job. I'm still a deputy -- but I'll be helpin' Herb Irwin at the jail, and sometimes Hershel Adrian as bailiff in court -- but my main job is somethin' else."

Presley Cross came back from Jules's office with a worried expression across his face.

"There something else already booked?" the bartender asked.

"Oh, no," Cross said. "It appears to be clear. I penciled in Judge Parker and the Bar Association at 8 PM."

"Good. I'll expect you then."

Cross hurried out of the bar.

"What got into him?" Stoney asked.

"Who knows," Mace said, enjoying his beer. "Tell me about this new job of yours."

CHAPTER 22

"**D**eputy Welch would like a word with you, Your Honor." Presley Cross spoke to Judge Parker as the judge left the courtroom to take the stairs up to his office.

"Welch?" the judge said feeling a headache coming on. "What does he want?"

"He didn't say. He returned from the scout with Marshal Truax and John Browneagle with a wagon full of prisoners yesterday. Perhaps it's about that."

"Give me a half-hour to eat in peace, then send him in," Judge Parker said, shaking his head as he headed upstairs.

When Welch's knock sounded on the door to the judge's chamber, Judge Parker had steeled himself for almost anything -- but what he got was totally unexpected.

"Your Honor," Welch said, standing hat in hand before the jurist's desk, "I come to offer my services."

"What? You're already a Deputy, Welch. You don't like that job?"

"Oh, it's fine. And Marshal Truax is going to be the right man fer that job. But I hear tell that when it comes to hanging', your jailer Herb Irwin don't know his butt from a barn door. Them two you've already strung up had an awful time a dyin'."

"Well, yes. There did seem to be some problems with that execution."

"That's what I wanted t' talk t' you about, Your Honor."

Judge Parker's head was almost spinning at what Stoney would possibly have to suggest -- but the judge motioned for the deputy to sit.

"You know I been hung by men who didn't know what th' hell they was doin' --," the judge nodded remembering how he first met Stoney astride his horse, hands tied behind him and rope around his neck, "-- still got th' scars t' remind me --," Stoney pulled down his neckerchief to display the permanent rope burns on his neck, "-- but there's somethin' you don't know. Back in th' war, my outfit caught a Yankee spy. We let him take a long drop off the edge of a railroad bridge with a short rope."

"All of this is leading to something, isn't it, Deputy?"

"Yes, sir. I've been almost hung -- and I did th' job of hangin' a spy myself once. When I did it -- it was quick and done in a snap. Not like the boys you strung up out here."

"I understand."

"What I'm sayin', Judge, is -- if a man's gotta' be hanged -- it ought t' be quick and done right." Stoney watched Judge Parker a moment and then said, "I think I could do that job -- and do it one hell of a lot better than it was done here last time."

"You're -- offering to -- take over the job of -- executioner?"

"'Hangman,' I'd call it. But yes. No matter what some ol' som'bitch done, if he's goin' t' be neck stretched -- it ought t' be quick --," Stoney snapped his fingers, "and that's that."

Judge Parker sat back in his chair considering the offer.

"Let me see -- as a deputy, you *are* an officer of the court -- and it could well be within your official *assigned* duties. You honestly understand what's supposed to be done?"

"The hangman's knot has thirteen loops around it, and one end slips through," he held up the piece of rope he'd been fooling' within his hands and demonstrated. "Fella' needs t' drop between 4 and 5 feet -- more than that, depending on how heavy he is -- the noose could pop his head right off. That's not what you want. The knot should be rested on the man's shoulder so when it yanks tight, it snaps his neck like a twig -- ain't supposed t' strangle him t' death."

"Deputy Welch, you've got yourself a job. But this won't be a full-time occupation. I'll find a couple of other duties to occupy your time."

"Well, not too many, Judge. Bein' the hangman means I'll need time t' prepare fer ever' one -- and some time off t' recover. I mean, this is goin' t' put a real strain on my *sensitive* nature."

The meeting in the big room at the Sidewheeler of the local Bar Association was the reading of thin-faced Rupert Dalby's official Presidential Appointment as Prosecuting District Attorney. Even Temple Houston politely applauded the announcement.

"My official duties," Dalby said, "will be to pursue murder charges against a half dozen accused felons only recently delivered to the court by our marshals. This will begin a new era of righteous justice implemented with dispatch. Criminals will soon discover they have no friends in Ft. Smith."

The two local newspaper editors were also in attendance and took copious notes of Dalby's stance on the law in the Western District of Arkansas.

"I will be appointing two assistant prosecutors," the new District Attorney proclaimed. "Men with a passion for justice and vigor to punish those who mistakenly believe this is a part of the country where injustice is the norm. I want men of virtue -- but filled with upright, moral anger."

Judge Parker caught the eye of Temple Houston after this remark. The white-dressed attorney nodded his head. He and Judge Parker understood each other.

The next morning, Mace was in his new office and had just sat down to get to know his surroundings.

Judge Parker had left a law book on the marshal's desk opened to the statute spelling out the powers, duties and responsibilities of a federal marshal. It was while he was reading this that Mace noticed his door filled with the figure of Bass Reeves.

Mace stood as the full mustached black man entered and removed his hat.

"If your offer is still open, Marshal, I'll be proud to take it."

Mace and Bass shook hands.

"I'm pleased to hear that. Let's get you sworn in."

Mace got Bass to repeat the words of the oath and then pulled out one of the badges he had taken with him in his vest from when Mr. Cross had presented him with the bag of badges from Judge Parker. Mace shined up the six-pointed star on his sleeve before pinning it on the new deputy.

"Truth is," Bass said, "my wife and I talked it over -- and I'm jest not that good a farmer. This job will help us out more than my sweating' and plowin'."

Mace laughed good-naturedly.

"I expect the same thing would be true of me. Now, let's

take a trip down to the mercantile and the gunsmith to see everything you'll need. How's your horse?"

"She's a good one."

"Then, after we get you whatever else you need, I need to introduce you to the livery -- your official business will be on our nickel. Folks will need to know who you are."

"And it's not going t' be any trouble?"

"If there is, we'll handle it together, Mr. Reeves."

"Bass, please, Marshal."

"Then, it's Mace, not Marshal to you."

"Thank you, sir."

The Court Clerk knocked on the open door frame.

"Mr. Cross," Mace said, looking up. "Come on in. Mr. Presley Cross, Court Clerk, meet Deputy Marshal, Mr. Bass Reeves."

Cross was surprised and took his spectacles down from the top of his head to make sure he was seeing a black man. Then with a smile, the clerk shook hands with the new deputy before turning to Mace.

"Judge Parker asked me to deliver these to you personally." There were two official documents he handed the marshal. "The judge requested that you take Deputy Welch in particular for the search warrant."

Examining the pages, Mace saw that the first was a search warrant for the "office of the Sidewheeler saloon in Ft. Smith, Arkansas.

"And if it proves fruitful," Cross said, "please execute the arrest warrant."

The second warrant was for Jules Henry Morgan.

Mace looked up and saw Cross leaving and heard him call from down the hall, "The Judge would also like for you to execute them both -- today."

"Well," Mace said, grabbing his hat, "let's go find Deputy Welch."

CHAPTER 23

Stoney had a late breakfast at Ma Loutzenhizer's Dinner Bell on 3rd Avenue. It was a no-nonsense bunkhouse style place to eat. One long table stretched from one end of the place to the other with a couple of single tables crammed into the corners. Ma was a well-fed widow in her 40's who served the basics and plenty of them.

"Marshal," the lady said, topping off Stoney's blue speckled cup.

"Ma," Mace said. "Brought you a new deputy -- Bass Reeves."

The lady looked over the big man in the checkered coat and a cross draw holster.

"Looks like he can hold his vittles," she said.

"Yes, ma'am," Bass said, removing his hat.

"You boys here to eat or talk?"

"We came to get Stoney," Mace said.

"Take him," Ma said. "Never knew such a skinny man who could eat me out of my kitchen."

"It's your own fault, Ma," Stoney said, getting up but

taking a last drink of his coffee. "Your cookin's better than mine -- or anybody else fer that matter."

"You bet ya'," Ma said with a hearty laugh.

Stoney left three nickels on the table.

"Bass Reeves?" Stoney said, and the two men shook hands. Bass nodded. "Yes, sir."

"Don't 'sir' me," Stoney repeated the often-used line of all enlisted men in the service of every army in the world. "I work fer a livin' just like you. What's up, Marshal?"

They stepped out the door before Mace explained.

"I don't understand," Stony said, looking at the search warrant. "What are we looking for?"

"I got the idea from Mr. Cross that you'd know if you saw it."

"That little man is creepy sometimes. Okay, let's go."

★★★

The doors to the Sidewheeler were closed as Mace, Stoney, and Bass crossed the wooden sidewalk and banged on the door.

"We're not open!" came the call from inside.

"Marshal Truax -- on official business!" Mace yelled back.

A few moments later, the sandy-haired barkeep and owner Jules Morgan pulled open the door.

"Marshal?" he said, standing there without his apron on but a broom in his hands.

"Jules," Mace said, "we have a search warrant -- for your office."

"My office? What in the hell for?"

"We need to come in."

Jules stepped back and allowed the three lawmen to enter. The chairs were upside down on the tabletops as Mace handed over the official document. The middle-aged man looked at the paper, shaking his head.

"The office is behind the bar. Doors at the far end there," he pointed out.

As the three lawmen trooped toward the office, Jules recognized Bass.

"Bass Reeves?"

"He's a new deputy," Mace said as his companions went on inside the office.

"He ought t' be a good one," Jules said. "What's up with all of this?" he asked as Stoney and Bass disappeared into his office.

"Some-bitch!" Stoney sounded surprised from inside the office.

Mace turned and joined the other two men. Jules propped his broom against the door and started toward the far end of the bar. He was met with Mace returning with a well-worn Confederate cap in his hand.

"What are you doin' with this, Jules?" Stoney said.

Jules stopped, closing his eyes as he sighed, and his shoulders fell.

Stoney said. "What the hell!"

"You have a lawyer?" Mace asked.

When Jules looked up, he was sadder and older somehow. "I think I can get one."

Jules younger second barkeep came in from the back room with a tray of glasses just then and stopped.

"Jules, you open?" came the voice of Temple Houston, stepping in the open door. "It's kind of early, isn't it?"

"There he is now," Jules said. "Temple, will you be my lawyer?"

"'Course I will. What's going on?"

Mace pulled out a set of handcuffs and put them on the bar owner.

"Jules Morgan, you're under arrest for attempted murder."

"Attempted murder of whom?" Temple asked.

"Me!" Stoney said, pulling his neckerchief aside and pointing to his neck scars.

"What is your evidence?" Temple demanded.

Mace held up the cap and tossed it to the attorney. Temple looked it over and then looked at the name "Welch" scratched into the leather hatband.

"The mob that tried to lynch me took that off me so they could get the rope around my neck."

"What do I do, Temple?" Jules asked.

"Go with them. I'll meet you in court when you're arraigned. We'll get the bond posted and get you out of there till the trial."

Jules went quietly with the lawmen. As the group was leaving, Temple looked back at the younger bartender.

"Billy Bob, take care of things here. I'll take care of Jules."

CHAPTER 24

B ass went with Mace and Stoney to escort Jules to jail.
After that, the Marshal took his new deputy to
Shadrack Granger, the gunsmith. Granger did a
courtesy check of both Bass's Colt .45 revolver and his '73
Winchester. Two boxes of ammunition, one .45 and one .44 -
70, were put on the Marshal's account.

"Our payroll is due in next week," Mace told the
merchant. "I expect to settle accounts then."

"Whenever it is convenient for you, Marshal."

"I appreciate your patience -- but I would like to bring my
office current as soon as possible."

"That would be appreciated, too," the gunsmith said.

The two lawmen's next stop was the mercantile.

"Mr. Howell Keeling," Mace said, making the introduc-
tion, "I'd like you to meet Deputy Marshal Bass Reeves."

Without any hesitation, the older man offered the new
deputy his hand.

"Sure," he said, "I've seen him around with other
deputies. Mr. Reeves, it's a pleasure to make your
acquaintance."

"I'd like him to be able to draw whatever supplies he might need -- charged to my office," Mace said.

"Of course. Anything you need, Deputy."

"Well," Bass said, glancing at Mace and saying, "some hardtack, beans, and coffee?"

Mace nodded.

"Delta," the older man called to his daughter who was stacking shelves of cans at the back of the store, "the Marshal is here with a new Deputy. Come meet him while I get what he needs."

Mace had to work to keep from beaming at the sight of this woman who had affected him in ways he didn't want to consider -- at least not yet seriously.

Delta wiped off her hands as she approached, her lovely smile already in place and focused on Mace.

"Mace," she said, "how are the new lodgings?"

"Uh -- fine -- wonderful." Turning to Bass, he said, "I've rented the upstairs as a place to live." Back to Delta, he said, "Thank you for all the items you added -- I certainly didn't expect any of that."

"Well, you could hardly do without a coffee pot, a few plates and glasses -- and the other furniture was all in storage, so you are welcome to everything. And father has a couple of houses for you to look at for your sister."

"Much obliged."

She offered her hand to Bass.

"Delta Wadsworth," she said. "I'm my father's only daughter."

"She lost her husband over a year ago," Mace explained.

"Ma'am," Bass said, noticing the looks the marshal and the mercantile owner's daughter had exchanged -- but he said nothing. "I'm sorry for your loss."

"Thank you, Mr. Reeves. Come to the counter, and we'll get you everything you need," Delta said.

Once behind the counter, Delta remarked, "We were certainly surprised to hear about the arrest of Mr. Morgan."

"News travels that fast?" Mace asked.

"Ft. Smith is still a small town, Marshal. Whatever news there is we often get and make up our minds about before either newspaper comes out."

"Here you go," Howell Keeling said, bringing a paper sack of freshly ground coffee along with three cans to his daughter. She bagged the items while her father made notes in his ledger.

"Are you leaving town directly?" Delta asked Bass.

"Yes, ma'am. Oh," he wrinkled his brow and turned to Mace, "Marshal, there's a man I've worked with before -- he's been a tumbleweed wagon driver and camp helper. His name is Tobe Pardee. I want to take him with me. I'll pay him out of my salary."

"Nothin' doin'," Mace said. "If you need him and you vouch for him, consider him hired."

"Thank you, Marshall," Bass said a little surprised.

"Mace," Delta said, handing the previsions to Bass, "are you going to come to the church social and barn dance Saturday night?"

"It would be a good place for you to meet many of the townfolk," the proprietor said. "Take Roger's Road East. It's at Slatt's farm. You can't miss it."

"I suppose I should," Mace said. "Saturday night?"

"The Presbyterians and the Methodist," Delta said, "are joining forces."

"I'll plan to be there."

"We'll look forward to it," Delta said and tried to turn away before the blush to her cheeks was fully evident.

"You come back, Deputy, whenever you need to."

"Thank you, sir."

"Mr. Keeling," Mace said, "Delta." He doffed his hat.

★★★

Bass filled his saddlebags after saddling his horse.

"What's your plan?" Mace asked him.

"Well, I was thinkin' -- gettin' in t' Younger Bend would be easier for Pardee and me if we had a couple of stolen horses. You wouldn't happen to have a couple of those around, would you?"

"What we do have are some horses whose brands nobody knows." Mace turned and called to the Ferrier, "Buster?"

Young Pettijohn was up in the hayloft and called down.

"Up here, Marshal."

"You know Bass Reeves, don't you?"

"I do. Bass," he said as a greeting.

"He's now a deputy."

"Good for him," Buster Pettijohn said, "and good for all of us. What do you need?"

"A couple of stolen horses. Could we rent some of those I saw in my books that have been sold to you by deputies who brought them in?"

"I've sold some," Buster said, propping up his pitchfork and climbing down the ladder from the loft. "But there are a couple left."

"How many," Mace asked Bass.

"Two or three."

The marshal turned back to Pettijohn who said, "I'll fix you up."

While the livery owner gathered the horses, Mace said to Bass, "What are you going to do if Buckholde and the others are not there?"

"I could hang around for a while -- restin' up the way outlaws do out there. If a couple of them are there, I'll try t' bring them in. If Buckholde has gone, I'll get on his trail. Together Pardee and I should be able to track him down."

"And if none of them are around and you can't get a lead on where they are?"

"We'll wait around a bit and come back if we come up empty-handed. But I got all three on my list now, and I *will* bring 'em in -- sooner or later."

"If you do come up dry, there will be other warrants here we can give you. From what I can tell, there's no shortage of 'em."

"We won't waste too much time, on this, Marshal. But we will give it some serious work."

"That's up to you, Bass. This isn't something anybody but the man on the trail can decide."

"Thank you, Marshal."

Outside, Pettijohn had a string of three horses ready for Bass. The Deputy took the lead rope, tipped his hat to both the ferrier and to Mace as he rode out.

CHAPTER 25

J ules was arraigned before Judge Parker in the afternoon session. But the saloon owner's case was the last to be addressed that day. The wagon load of prisoners brought in by Deputy Welsh was all dealt with first. Make-believe-preacher Rosco Dury, thin-framed Ace Keogh, and saggy headed Will Hoxie -- the horse thieves and cowboy killers -- former slave Uziel Washington, the murder of his former owners, Ottis and Lutie Vanderhoff -- prostitute slayer and former marshal Bart Zolan -- were all charged with murder and given no bail.

Judge Parker did, however, set a $500 bond on Jules after the saloon owner was assigned a trial date. Temple paid the bond, and a very subdued Jules was released into the custody of his lawyer.

The series of murder trials began two days later. First up was former slave Uriel Washington. The trial lasted only for the morning session. Both of Uriel's companions, former slaves themselves named Israel and Buford, willingly gave eyewitness testimony to the murders of Ottis and Lutie Vanderhoff -- Uziel's former owners. The pair also admitted that Uziel had said at other times that he had been reasonably treated by the couple and ate as well as they did.

Still, they described how Uziel bashed in Ottis's head because the man had no job to offer Uziel nor money to pay him. Likewise, they told how Uziel had killed Lutie Vanderhoff with a hatchet.

Having no real defense, Uziel was convicted by the jury and sentenced to hang by Judge Parker.

Former Marshal Bart Zolan's trial began after lunch with Temple Morgan serving as his attorney. Whore house madam "Big Maude" Merritt had made the journey from Muskogee to Ft. Smith as promised to bare witness against Zolan. She wore a bright red dress, which was conservative in that it didn't display her significant breasts nor their cleavage. Judge Parker asked that she put down her pipe before taking the witness oath.

It was clear to everyone in the court that the prosecutor, Rupert Dalby, very much disliked having to rely on Big Maude as his key witness. He got her to tell her story as quickly as possible, and then Dalby took his seat.

"It appears to me," Temple said before he even stood, "that all your testimony, Miss Merritt, is circumstantial."

"What does that mean?" she asked, squinting at the lawyer.

"You testified that the victim, Miss Tollie Fredricks, willingly went to room number --," Temple looked at his notes, "-- eight."

"She did. But she didn't go there to get killed!"

"For the sake of propriety," Temple said, getting to his feet, "we'll not discuss why she went with the former marshal nor what took place in that room."

"He come for a poke -- like he always done," Maude said, and the jury burst into laughter.

Judge Parker pounded his gavel, "Order in the court! The witness will confine her answers to direct questions by the defense and nothing else."

"Yes, Your Honor," Big Maude said only slightly apologetically.

"As a point of fact, you cannot say what took place in that room, can you? You weren't there, and you didn't personally observe what took place."

"Well, no. But Bart Zolan took Tollie and a bottle of whiskey with him. I don't think they were having a tea party. That's not why men come to Big Maude's."

Again the jury laughed. And again, the judge gaveled them back to order.

"Well," Temple resumed, "they could have had a tea party for all you know. You were not there and didn't observe what took place."

"I can tell you that with a bottle of whiskey and a girl like Tollie, Zolan might have gotten so drunk he couldn't even get up to his main business."

Bart Zolan blushed as the jury laughed once more.

"Be that as it may -- all you can truly testify to is that Mr. Zolan and Miss Fredricks went into that room together -- there was a shot -- and when the door was opened, he was gone and she was dead. Isn't that true?"

"Yeah. That's what I've been saying'."

"No, Miss Merritt, you are claiming that my client shot the victim. You didn't see that. In fact, when the door was opened, Mr. Zolan wasn't even there, was he?"

"No. But his vest with his badge on it sure as hell was! Explain that some other way."

"Isn't it possible -- I'm saying *possible* -- that Bart Zolan could have taken his bottle with him and left room number eight -- by the window -- and after he was gone -- having forgotten his vest -- someone else snuck into that room and murdered Miss Fredricks?"

Big Maude made a puzzled face before she said, "It is also possible that the Big Bad Wolf kidnapped Bart and the wolf shot Tollie -- but I sure as hell doubt it!"

The jury was slapping their knees and howling as Temple told the judge, "No more questions of this witness, Your Honor."

In the end, for all of Temple's imagined possibilities and lack of eye witness testimony, the jury found Bart Zolan guilty, and he, too, was sentenced to hang by the neck until he was dead.

CHAPTER 26

M ace and Delta were becoming an *item* around town. Especially after the barn dance. The pair often danced together, although both were in demand by others in town throughout the evening. From his years as an Army officer, Mace had become an adept dancer, as was Delta. He had learned from his sister in at the military functions on the posts where they shared officer housing. Mace and Delta both took several turns around the barn with different partners. But it was evident to any who cared to look that there was something special between the widow and the marshal.

After that night, it was quietly known that the attractive widow was the prize already won by Mace. Still, they kept everything respectful and above board. The unspoken understanding that she felt for the Marshal kept other would-be suitors at bay from Delta.

Mace had dinner with Delta and her father at their house occasionally, but he had yet to kiss Delta or even take her in his arms. She would have welcomed his advances.

For Mace, this was a new experience. No woman had ever

touched his heart the way Delta had -- and he wasn't absolutely sure of what to do with these feelings. Marriage and a family had never been future prospects he envisioned for himself. Now, when he was alone, he found he was imaging such things.

There was much more paperwork involved in being marshal than Mace had believed at first. He discovered that his predecessor, Bart Zolan, had not only neglected most of it but had allowed the bulk of the red tape to fall on the Court Clerk. Little by little, Mace was able to get Presley Cross to open up and trust that Mace would do the job he had been appointed to do.

The payroll did come in, and it involved two months' worth of cash and back payments. Mace worked his way through the ledger until all the figures balanced.

He also met about a third of the current force of deputies. They all seemed to know already that Mace had been out with John Browneagle and was somewhat acquainted with the outlaw world in the Indian Territory. He learned other tidbits -- such as from which merchants across the 70,000 square miles of their responsibility the marshals could expect fair and honest dealing.

He decided to make an appointment with banker Cordell Broyles, president of The National Bank of Arkansas. The man he met in his wood-paneled office was in his 40's. He had a prominent belly from enjoying the good life. He sported thin mutton chops and chin whiskers.

Seated in the banker's plush office, the older man asked, "What can the National Bank of Arkansas do for you, Marshal?"

"I'd like to set up a system whereby each deputy marshal can draw up to $50 in cash each month against his salary."

"Cash?" the banker asked amazed. "You have what -- over a hundred deputy marshals?"

"And I plan to fill the roster up to my quota of 200."

"At $50 each, that would be possibly a thousand dollars every month."

"I'm glad we agree. An understanding of math seems to be something we share."

"Well, obviously, you don't share an understanding of what such a disbursal of funds would mean to the bank, Marshal."

"As I understand it, you receive the federal payroll for Judge Parker's court."

"We do."

"And you don't pay out cash until a federal employee presents his voucher. This is true of both federal employees and merchants with whom we have accounts."

"Correct."

"Which means you are not paying out all the money you receive. There is a substantial sum which you hold onto until the claimant presents the voucher -- frequently months after the date in which you've received the funds from the government."

"Yes, that's true."

"And during the interim, you use the cash to make investments, loans -- all making a profit for the bank."

"A bank is not in business to become financially unstable, Marshal. We have investors ourselves. It is our fiduciary duty to make use of what funds we have on hand to increase the value for our investors."

"And helping our deputy marshals -- who go out and risk their lives to keep your institution and the Territory safe -- would be not only an inconvenience but a drain of the available capital you have on hand?"

"You do grasp the situation very well, indeed."

"The question is, Mr. Broyles, do you?" Mace asked. "What kind of security do you think this bank -- any bank in town or the Territory would enjoy without the Marshal's Service?"

"Are you threatening me, Marshal?"

"Merely pointing out the obvious -- which you tend to ignore when it is not in your interest, Mr. Broyles."

The banker mulled over his exchange with Mace before he pursed his thin lips and leaned his elbows on his big desk.

"We have no obligation to offer such a service. We have been asked to safeguard the government's money and pay it out as demanded."

"I'm requesting a new service."

"I don't see how we can oblige, Marshal. We are the largest bank for 150 miles in any direction. I don't believe you are in any position to make such a request -- nor am I in a position to honor it. I don't consider it part of our duty."

Mace got to his feet.

"Perhaps the Wells Fargo company, which I understand is going into the banking business, would see it differently."

"We have the contract with the court, Marshal."

"I have the ear of Judge Parker. Do you want to bet you can convince him that my request is somehow out of line?"

Broyles' face fell.

"You wouldn't."

"Why wouldn't I? If we're not getting the service we require from this bank -- our funds would certainly be a benefit to a new institution like Wells Fargo -- perhaps enough to make them the largest bank in 150 miles."

Broyles licked his lips.

"Uh -- what if we could -- somehow manage to -- uh -- meet your request with a limit of $25?"

"You've never been out in the Territory and in need of

cash have you, Mr. Broyles? It's something my deputies face every day. Fifty dollars."

"Thirty -- thirty-five."

"Fifty."

The banker was smart enough to know when he had met his match.

"In return for this," he finally said, "I expect some additional service from your men."

"You have your bank security force," Mace said.

"Yes, but the presence of deputy marshals would do us a world of good."

"All right," Mace said, offering his hand, which the sweating banker took quickly.

"Agreed. When can I expect to see your men?"

"That will be up to them. They will come to draw money as they see the need."

"I mean for protection."

"Oh, well, you are free to expect them at any time."

"And when will they be available?"

"I doubt they ever will be."

"You just agreed, Marshal. We shook on it."

"Our agreement, Mr. Broyles, was that you could *expect* my deputies to provide additional security. You are absolutely free to do that. Expect them all you like. But that's not a part of their duties."

Mace walked out, leaving the banker with his mouth open.

CHAPTER 27

Seventeen-year-old cowboy, Dell Maguire, had ridden up to Ft. Smith from his job at an East Texas lumber mill. The young rider had taken work there hoping the U.S. marshals would track down the killers of his cowboy companions months earlier. Dell was the only survivor of the slaughter of the cowpunchers' night camp as they headed back to Texas from Missouri. The day the telegram came from Presley Cross that the killer had been caught, Dell mounted up and rode to Ft. Smith to testify.

At the trial, the youngster looked older than his teen years because of what he had experienced and the anger inside him toward the men who slaughtered his friends.

Make-believe-preacher Rosco Dury cleaned himself up and slicked back his hair for the trial. But quickly, as Dell described the bloody night around the campfire, the jury began to see through Rosco's demeanor. Thin framed Ace Keogh, and shaggy headed Will Hoxie didn't know how even to pretend to be anything other than the soulless killers they were.

Even taking the stand and trying his best to sway the jury

with his silver tongue, Rosco succeeded only in ensuring he and his partners would end up at the end of a rope. Although the trial took a full afternoon, the jury reached its verdict in less than a half-hour. These three would join Uziel Washington and Bart Zolan on the gallows.

The trial for attempted murder for Jules Morgan appeared to be an easy win for Rupert Dalby. The stern and unforgiving prosecutor told the jury about the attempted lynching of now Deputy Marshal, Stoney Welch, and the discovery of Stoney's Confederate cap in Jules' office. He even went over Stoney's words when he testified. Dalby made a point of honest men not living by the law of the gun but the law and the courts -- not by the will of men who rode at night and were vigilantes -- men who wore hoods to hide their faces.

Temple Houston did not put Jules on the stand in his own defense and had very little evidence or testimony to convince the jury of Jules' innocence. It all came down to his closing argument. After Dalby's blazing condemnation of vigilante justice and the obvious connections between Stoney's testimony about the thief who took his cap before someone else put a rope around his neck, the prosecution rested.

Temple waited for Rupert to sit before he got to his feet. He approached the jury in his white suit, vest, shirt, and tie. The defense case and Jules' fate hung of the words of Temple's spoke next.

"Gentlemen," he began, "think about this for a second. Everything that you've heard in this trial -- all the evidence -- and the testimony is circumstantial. That means there are events and pieces of evidence which have been strung together by the prosecution to prove that Jules Morgan -- a man most of you know -- to be at least an accomplice to an *attempted* killing. But remember, no one died in this case. There was no murder. And even the prosecution's star witness -- the would-be victim of the crime Mr. Dalby would have you believe took place -- cannot identify my client as one of the men involved in his abduction and -- again -- *attempted* lynching."

Temple studied the faces of the dozen men in the jury box before he continued.

"As any rancher knows, the killing of a cow from his herd isn't necessarily the work of a mountain lion. The deed could well have been done by a bear, a wolf -- even a pack of coyotes. So with no evidence that it was Jules Morgan who committed this crime -- it would be a miscarriage of justice to assign it to a man who happened to have possession of the cap which once belonged to Deputy Marshal Welch. Gentlemen, don't make that leap from circumstances to positively blaming a crime which didn't amount to murder -- to a man none of us can connect to the event in question."

Temple allowed his words and ideas to hang in the air as he crossed away from the jury and stopped at the defense table. He looked down at his notes a moment and then turned back to the jury again.

"Many of you men were here before His Honor Judge Parker came. Yet, in those years we had all the pieces of the system we depend upon for justice -- but with Judge Parker's predecessor -- who we all know resigned his post to keep from being brought up on charges of corruption -- and with Bart Zolan as U.S. Marshal -- what we had in Ft. Smith and in the Indian Territory was not law and order -- and it certainly was not justice."

There was agreement pretty much through the jury. But Temple Houston wasn't finished. He pressed on.

"What is justice, after all? It isn't revenge -- it isn't vengeance. It is an attempt to bring equality and fairness among men -- so that we can live in peace. It is not '*an eye for an eye*' -- it is a way to administer laws we have come to agree upon -- from the 10 Commandments to the Golden Rule -- from petty crimes to capital offenses. Impartial -- all men equal in the eyes of the law -- no favorites, no one privileged, no one above the law -- all of us the same.

"But what happens when the system breaks down? What do we do when the judge is corrupt -- the marshal a bully and just no good?"

Once more, Temple allowed his words and ideas to make their way into the consciousness of each man on the jury.

"When society has reached that point -- and we all know what that's like because we've seen it right here in our river city and the territory on West. This is the time when men of principle -- men of courage -- men with consciences -- do what we know is wrong for the right reasons. I am talking about vigilantes."

Mummers were heard from the gallery and from the jury.

"We know vigilantism is wrong -- but when the law -- when justice breaks down -- what are we to do? But vigilante committees -- like juries -- are made up of men -- men who make mistakes. Sometimes horrible mistakes.

"In the very first case I tried in this court -- with Deputy Marshal Stoney Welch as my client -- the jury found him guilty of murder -- a murder the evidence could not prove. Nevertheless, the jury, mostly angry at me, voted to convict Mr. Welch -- and only the justice of His Honor, Judge Parker, overruled them and dismissed the charges. This was true justice shown then -- when men of goodwill were willing to make a terrible mistake.

"Well, it is possible that vigilantes can make mistakes, too. We are told that vigilante justice is no justice -- that vigilantes make many mistakes. But we know of miner's courts and other forms of unofficial justice, which are the only ones who can act in the public will. Now that we have a working justice system -- we all agree vigilante justice is not for us. But we also know that sometimes justice comes out of the barrel of a gun when a marshal or his deputies -- or one of the Indian Policemen -- have no choice but to settle matters with gun smoke.

"All of this is to say that -- first of all -- there's no actual proof Jules Morgan was one of the men trying to lynch a man many in this town thought was a killer -- we know now it was a mistake.

"The cap found in Jules' office -- how did that get there? I saw the new marshal, before he was a marshal, hand Jules a bowie knife and a pistol -- and ask him not to return it to two men who would have killed themselves in a drunken fight. Many things get left in any bar -- the Sidewheeler is no exception -- and no one can say for sure how Deputy's Welch's cap ended up in Jules' office.

"With or without that item, there is no proof that Jules Morgan had anything to do with the crime -- remember that crime didn't end up killing anyone.

"Lastly, justice is now in your hands, gentlemen. There is much to consider. It's more than circumstantial evidence -- no eye witness testimony -- and the law says that just because a man does not testify on his behalf that you cannot let that lead you to believe therefore he is guilty. What is justice in the case? You must decide -- and be willing to live with your decision.

"Your Honor, the defense rests."

The jury found Jules innocent, and Judge Parker dismissed all charges. There was clapping in the courtroom. Few saw Jules after he thanked his lawyer step over to Deputy Welch and humbly say, "We were very wrong, Stoney. I ask you for your forgiveness."

Stoney rubbed the scars on his neck before he nodded his head. "I've made some mistakes in my life, too, Jules."

"Thank you," Jules said. "And remember, your money's no good in the Sidewheeler if you ever decide to come back. For the rest of your life, you'll drink free."

"Now there's an idea," Stoney smiled and shook hands with Jules.

CHAPTER 28

At exactly 9 AM, on a Friday, September 3rd, 1875, Deputy Marshal Stoney Welch, along with four armed jail guards, led Uriel Washington, Bart Zolan, Rosco Dury, Ace Keogh, Will Hoxie, and Big Indian, Knut Marble, from the jail to specially constructed gallows. Each convicted man was positioned over a trap door in the 20 foot long, 14-foot high platform.

Bailiff Hershel Adrian read the charges against each man, and then the signed death warrants for them one by one. While this was going on, Stoney was tying the knees and legs of each man who could only stand and wait. When the last man was secured, Stoney stepped up to each and asked if he had any last words. Only Rosco Dury spoke.

"Are you going t' hang us or talk us t' death?"

"You'll be dead in just a minute," Stoney promised.

The jail yard was crowded with every person who could squeeze into a place where the hanging was visible. It was something of a carnival atmosphere with an occasional laugh heard from the throng. One man had his two 5 and 6-year-old sons upon his shoulders. This was to be a hard lesson he was sure they'd never forget -- instructions to live their lives down the "straight and narrow" path.

The hanging deputy placed a black burlap bag over each man's head before slipping the noose around his neck and positioning the hangman's knot on his left shoulder. When Stoney reached Rosco, the outlaw said, "I don't need a blindfold or a bag!"

"This ain't fer you," Stoney said. "This is so we don't have to look at you when your neck snaps and you piss yourself and shit your pants." With that, the deputy jerked the bag over Rosco's head and applied the noose.

As Stoney surveyed his work, he nodded to himself and stepped over to a long lever, which stuck through a notch in the floor from below. He looked across at the jail door where Mace stood with his arms crossed over his chest. Mace nodded his assent.

With a swift and firm jerk, Stoney yanked the lever. All the trap doors opened, and six men fell as the crowd gasped. All the condemned abruptly came to the end of their ropes. Big Indian twitched once, but none of the others moved beyond swaying in the air from the momentum of their sudden stop from their fall.

The crowd was hushed as all six men dangled with the black bags over their heads. One teenager pointed out the wet spot that suddenly grew on the apex of Bart Zolan's pants. There were a few snickers, and a couple of people vomited, but mostly the people just silently drifted away.

One of the jail guards retrieved an open wagon with six empty coffins from behind the jail. Then together, the other guards untied the loose end of the ropes from under the gallows and lowered the bodies into the wooden boxes. Stoney collected the black bags and coiled up the hemp nooses.

Noticeably absent from the event was Judge Parker. As

usual, he never attended the executions. His job was done, he believed when he followed the law and sentenced the convicted murderers and rapists to death.

The two newspaper editors both were still scratching notes and observations as the event concluded, and the bodies of the executed were driven off. Mace decided he had supervised everything he was even remotely responsible for -- so he walked across the beaten-down grass, out the street and down to the mercantile. He took the outside stairs and went up to his rooms to be alone. What he'd just been a part of needed some thinking.

Sitting in the rocking chair Delta had put in his living room, Mace sat and rocked. All six of the men who were just hanged were killers. They'd been tried and convicted by a jury of their peers, found guilty, and sentenced to death.

Ft. Smith and the Territory -- the whole world as far as that went -- were better off without any of those men still in it. They had died easier than any of the men and women they'd killed. Mace had no doubts about any of that.

If anything, the spectacle of six murders being executed at once would shout loud and clear that law and order -- and he hoped, justice -- were back. For that he was glad.

It wasn't the first time he'd seen men die -- nor was it the first time he'd had a hand in their killing. As a Ranger and as an officer in the Army, he knew death and had dealt in it. Did he have the mark of Cain on him? Was that mark the ability to take human lives?

Delta deserved better than that.

Mace took the inside stairs down to the mercantile's backroom, used his key, and unlocked the door. He opened it, but before he could step from the landing to the storeroom, he heard Howell Keeling say, "This is a $100 dollar gold piece, Mister. I can't change that."

Mace stopped and didn't move a muscle.

Closer to him, he heard Delta saying, "Will there be anything else, Miss?"

An unknown woman said, "No. That will do."

"Let me put this up on the counter with the other purchases," Delta said." Then Delta's delicate steps could be heard crossing the floor followed by the boots of someone who was light on their feet -- a woman?

"Oh, I was just funin' ya'," the man's voice said at the counter.

Mace removed his hat and eased back so he could see through the crack between the door and its frame. At the counter talking to Delta's father was a tall man wearing a new hat and boots, a set of saddlebags slung over his shoulder. He picked up the gold coin from the counter and put it back inside a bag within one of the saddle bags. From his pocket, he produced a considerable pile of greenbacks and counted out his payment with those.

The woman who had joined the man wore a riding dress and a hat, held in place by a string around her chin. A shorter and thinner man also joined the pair at the counter.

"Delta," Howell Keeling said, "would you see if you can find us an empty box or two for these folks.

"Yes, Father," she said.

Mace waited for Delta to arrive at the open door. She started to say something when he grabbed her and pulled her to him, kissing her full on the lips.

Delta was taken aback but slipped her arms around Mace just as he pulled back and put a single finger to his lips.

"Shhhhhh," he whispered.

"Oh, we don't need boxes," the woman at the counter said. We can put everything in the wagon then go get something to drink."

"Good idea," the bigger man said.

"Don't say a word," Mace said quietly, leaning back and peaking through the crack. "Are there any more customers in the store?"

Delta shook her head.

"As soon as these three are gone, call your father back here. And stay here until I come to get you!" he ordered her.

The three customers, their purchases in their arms, walked out the open double doors and crossed the wooden sidewalk to the street.

"Call him," Mace said.

"Father?" Delta called, still not understanding.

As soon as her father arrived, "Saying, Delta, why is this door ...."

Mace left Delta and stepped out, moving past a perplexed proprietor. He walked to the open doors and watched as the trio left the back of their wagon parked in front of the store to head up the street where the saloons were.

Mace stepped down into the dirt and called, "Emmitt Buckholde! Doc Kellen! Bell Starr! Stop! Put your hands up, and don't move! You're under arrest for robbery and murder!"

The three stopped. Mace noticed for the first time that they all were armed, even Bell.

Mace had his pistol in his hand and cocked it so they would hear the click of his hammer locked into place ready to fire.

"Use your left hands to unbuckle your gunbelts and let them slide to the ground." For a moment, none of them moved. "Do it! Now!!" Mace commanded.

The trio slowly raised their hands.

"Gunbelts!" Mace repeated as the streets cleared.

The three did as they were told. Both Doc Kellen and Bell Starr's weapons and belts dropped into the dirt. Emmitt Buckholde's belt and pistol dropped, but he had his holster tied down and a thong around the hammer of his Schofield pistol.

"Can I use my hand to untie my holster?" he asked calmly.

"Turn around," Mace said, and Buckholde did, his rig dangling from his tie-down. "Lift your leg and *slowly* untie it!" Mace ordered him.

Emmitt followed Mace's direction lifting his right foot off the ground before he reached down and pulled on the slip knot with his right hand. The gun rig dropped to the street.

But as Buckholde straightened up, he raised his right hand a little faster than he needed to. From the slit behind his buttoned cuff, a small pistol swung up on a metal arm right into his palm. Buckholde cocked and fired the .32 caliber pistol.

Mace heard the bullet rip through the air right by his head as he fired his revolver. His shot caught Buckholde in the saddlebags which had swung across his chest. Mace's shot slammed into the bag and pushed the outlaw back but not off his feet.

Buckholde cocked his small pistol for a second shot, but Mace was quicker and shot the killer in the breastbone right above the tilted saddlebags. The outlaw hit the ground dead.

Both Doc Kellen and Bell Starr stooped to get their guns when the clear sound of levered Winchesters was heard close by. The two froze.

Mace had cocked his Smith and Wesson .44 Russian again but didn't have to fire. He saw it was Bass Reeves and John Browneagle, who stood rifles in hand aimed at the outlaw pair.

Stepping over to Buckholde, Mace saw the hide-away rig

the killer had used. The second shot was half-cocked, and Mace lifted it out of the dead man's fist. He pulled the saddle-bags off of Buckholde and checked the contents. Both sides contained a cloth bag of gold coins.

"Want us to see these two t' jail, Marshal," Bass said, moving in on the contrite bandits.

"When did you get back, Bass?"

"Followed these three when they came in to watch th' hangin'. Stopped by and got John to come into town with me."

"I'm glad you did. Thank you -- both. And yes. Please take them to jail."

Browneagle and Bass ushered Kellen and Bell toward the jail. The pair had their hands back up as they moved out.

Mace picked up all three gunbelts and said, "Somebody gets the undertaker."

A couple of boys, 11 and maybe 12, ran off together racing to do what the Marshal had ordered.

Mace had holstered his gun and pick up Buckholde's new hat. He brought it along with the saddlebags and gunbelts to the wooden sidewalk. When he looked up, Delta and her father were standing in the doorway to their store. Mace gave the hat to Howell.

"I'm afraid all the things they bought were paid for with stolen money."

The older man nodded and took the hat before crossing to the wagon to retrieve the other purchases.

Delta bent down and tore off a piece of her petticoat. She wadded it up and held it beside his head. "You're bleeding, Mace."

He touched his ear and pulled back his fingers with blood on them. Buckholde had come close to killing Mace with the one-shot he got off.

Mace sighed and looked up at Delta.

"When you see me -- you must see Cain -- or Pontius Pilate. A killer just like him," Mace pointed to Buckholde's body in the street.

Delta cupped Mace's face in her hand and leaned down to look him directly in the eyes.

"What I see, Mace Truax is David willing to stand against Goliath -- I see Sampson. I see a man who does what others cannot -- or will not." She smiled and kissed him quickly. Then she said, "I also see the father of my children."

THE END

THANK YOU

Thank you for taking the time to read <u>The Gavel and the Gun</u> . If you enjoyed it, please consider posting a short review on line at the site where you purchased the book and telling your friends. Word of mouth is an author's best friend and much appreciated. I love to write these stories, but it's even better to sell some and to know other people take some joy from them, too.

If you're interested is subscribing to my monthly newsletter, contact me at jacks@wrightbridgepress.com. You know when my next novel is coming out and a little bit about how I work. I would love to hear from you.

Thank you,

Jack R. Stanley

TO GET TWO FREE E-NOVELS
BY
JACK R. STANLEY

ChroniclesMURDER IN MULESHOE
There's a killer in town. Do we hunt the S.O.B. down or
throw him a parade?

GUNS ALONG THE RIO
Two fresh-off-the-ranch 17-year-olds join the Texas Rangers in
1858. What could possibly go wrong?

Go To http://eepurl.com/dKEi_Y

ABOUT THE AUTHOR

Jack R. Stanley is a native Texan born two blocks inside Texas and raised six blocks inside Arkansas in Texarkana, Arkansas/Texas. He received his B.F.A. from Texas Christian University in Ft. Worth in Radio-TV-Film. As an officer in the U.S. Army serving in Vietnam as a TV-Film Director, he was awarded the Bronze Star. He says when you're in a fire-fight and you have a camera when everybody else on both side have guns, you get to change your pants a lot.

After his military service he earned both his M.A. and his Ph.D. at the University of Michigan in Ann Arbor in Radio-TV-Film. He also received two of Michigan's most presti-gious creative writing awards, The Hopwood Award, one for a one-act play and the second for a novel. His novel, <u>Campus Confidential</u> is available to Amazon.com in paperback.

Stanley's first academic position was TV Area Head at The University of Texas at Austin's Department of Radio-TV-Film. He later moved to deep south Texas and the Lower Rio Grande Valley for a challenging position with The University of Texas-Pan American. Here he taught Theatre-TV-Film for 30 years in the Department of Communication serving as Department Chair at U.T.P.A. for 11 years. He did take one year out to work for The University of Alaska Anchorage as a visiting professor. Back in Texas, Stanley directed for stage at The University Theatre, produced and directed fifteen student staffed, cast, and crewed feature films, writing most of the original screenplays. A very few of his credits are available on IMDB.com.

Stanley, 50 years happily married to his high school sweetheart, now lives in the Texas Panhandle where he writes his fiction and runs his blog, *www.TheFictionWritersNotebook.com*. His e-mail address is. jack.stanley@utrgv.edu

ALSO BY THE AUTHOR:

Novels

[Westerns]

Guns Along The Rio

West Of The Frio

A Hard Line Between The Rios

The Mormon Marshal

The Gavel and the Gun

Incident At Lajitas

Pancho's Pilot

Occurance At Latigo

Return To Redemption

Some Men Need Killin'

[Political Fiction]

The Reluctant President

The Reluctant Incumbent

The Reluctant Candidate

[Vietnam]

Through A Lens Darkly: Vietnam

[Mysteries]

Murder In Muleshoe

Corpse In Canyon

The Lovecraft Murders

Short Stories

TALES FROM THE ALASKAN GOLD RUSH

Klondike Justice

Dangerous Camp On The Kenai

The Winds of Skagway

Screenplays

6 and 10

The 7th Luger

Afternoon Delight

Angel's Revenge

Between Love And Murder

Blood Drive

Death Scene

The Defection of Grigori Dorsky

The Evil Eye

Fatty and Hearst

Gideon: The Horse That Saved Texas

Hell In Paradise

Hollowpoint

Holiday For An Assassin

Horse Thief Hollow

Incident At Lajitas

Love, Lust, & Life

Mom & Apple Pye

Pancho's Pilot

The Prometheus Peril

The Rape of Sarah Quinn

Reservations

River of Tears

Seven Reasons Why

The Thing About Love

The Texas Rattlesnake Murders

Too Good To Be True

The Vampire Rose

A Violent End

The Virgin Casanova

Plays

Antigone In Texas

Cyrano

The Last Virgin From Las Vegas

The Seven Keys

The Unwed Widow

www.ingramcontent.com/pod-product-compliance
Lightning Source LLC
Chambersburg PA
CBHW032209170626
46808CB00006B/2394